The Roof Beneath Their Feet

GEETANJALI SHREE has written four novels – *Mai, Tirohit, Hamara Shahar Us Baras,* and *Khali Jagah* – and six collections of short stories in Hindi, besides a monograph – *Between Two Worlds: An Intellectual Biography of Premchand* – in English. Some of her fiction has been translated into English, French, German, Serbian, Czech, Japanese, Gujarati, Bangla, Oriya, Malayalam, and Urdu. The English translation of *Mai* won the Sahitya Academy Award, and was shortlisted for the Hutch-Crossword Translation Award. She has received the Krishna Baldev Vaid Sammaan, Hindi Akademi Sahityakar Sammaan, Dwijdev Sammaan, and Indu Sharma Katha Sammaan for her contribution to Hindi literature. The English translation of *Khali Jagah* was longlisted for the DSC Prize for South Asian Literature 2013.

RAHUL SONI is a writer, editor and translator. He has edited *Home from a Distance* (Pratilipi Books, 2011), an anthology of Hindi Poetry in English translation, and translated *Magadh* (Almost Island Books, 2013), a collection of poems by Shrikant Verma. He was a Charles Wallace Visiting Fellow in Literary Translation at the University of East Anglia in 2010, and received the Sangam House Fellowship in 2012. He lives in India.

Praise for the Book

'One of the finest Hindi writers, Geetanjali has created for herself a thoughtful, lyrical and contemporary fictional world, which is free from moral posturing and political hectoring. And Rahul Soni's English translation of *Tirohit* is attentive to its poetic nuances and intelligently responsive to its complexity'

– Alok Bhalla

'Intense, intriguing, unorthodox in her language, Geetanjali's every novel is a delectable treat'

– Nivedita Menon

'This is a playful, suggestive and lyrical work of fiction in the best traditions of the modern Indian novel. She 'plays' language and memory like musical instruments. Words construct her text while the silences constitute the subtext. The roof in the novel becomes a space, something like the virtual world, where alternative lives are played out, and instinct and imagination break free of fragile social mores and conventions. Liberatingly uninhibited and intensely poetic'

– K. Satchidanandan

The Roof Beneath
Their Feet

Geetanjali Shree

Translated from the Hindi by
Rahul Soni

HARPER**PERENNIAL**

An Imprint of HarperCollins *Publishers*

First published in English in India in 2013 by Harper Perennial
An imprint of HarperCollins *Publishers*
First published in Hindi as *Tirohit* in 2001 by Rajkamal Prakashan
Building No 10, Tower A, 4th Floor, DLF Cyber City, Phase II,
Gurugram – 122002
www.harpercollins.co.in

1 2 3 4 5 6 7 8 9 10

ISBN: 978-93-5029-619-6

Typeset in 10/14 Palatino
Jojy Philip New Delhi 110 015

I

Walls have ears, but alas they can't speak – the people living under this roof lamented – or they would have told such stories about the secret goings-on of the mohalla! So telling stories now fell to people who, unlike walls, had too much tongue and not enough ears. And eyes, still fewer. But because they could speak, such failings didn't matter; stories were created, stories were told. They even started coming true! They echoed in the wind that swept the rooftops, and could be seen through the kaleidoscopic cobwebs in the skylight.

And was it not on this very rooftop where it all began? Where the children of the mohalla played, copycatting one another, and bounding from the reproofs of adults. Shouting 'times' for no reason, they would run to the skylight to peep, and start giggling nervously. I, too, would run with them to peep into the room, and the older children would pull at my shorts and threaten,

'Tell us –
Did you see what we just saw?
Wham bam, wham bam going on!'

Clutching at my shorts, I would shout,

'Yes, I saw what you just saw!
Wham bam, wham bam going on!'

And with the 'wham bam, wham bam', I'd rock my head

from side to side, which would make them laugh, and I would laugh with them and return to throwing pebbles and hopping on one leg.

The older children wouldn't return to playing after they had peeped, though. The ancient, grimy, cracked skylight was like a magical glass, filtered through which, stories turned into swings that the adults would then ride higher and higher on the rooftop, adding their inflamed whispers to the wind that swept through the mohalla.

Did you see? they asked. Even the children have seen! And children don't lie, do they? They're pure of heart, aren't they? So they'd build walls around what they wanted to believe. When they looked down the skylight, didn't they see Uncle and Lalna sleeping in the big room, and poor Chachcho sleeping alone in the room by the porch?

Was it possible? I wondered, trying to remember the two rooms near the porch, neither of which could be seen from the skylight. One of them was the library. The other was the storeroom, stuffed with a world full of old and broken things to be sold as scrap or to be given away to servants. An old daybook, notebooks from school, the broken recliner which, with a newspaper under it, had served as a commode by Uncle's bed in the early stages of his sickness, boxes, bottles, tin cans, pens that didn't work, an old fridge crammed with burlap bags, a cage, a rattrap, a tattered holdall, the new brass pichkari bought on Holi, which looked very grand, but was useless when it came to squirting colour – it shot out a thin trickle and was, therefore, soon relegated to a corner of the store, away from festivities – some rope, a trowel, a broken pot and a leaking pitcher. All the children of the mohalla wanted to hide in the storeroom while playing hide and seek, but hiding there meant getting an earful from Lalna and a smacking from their parents.

I felt sad. Was it from remembering the storeroom? Or the books in the library?

'So, there was a library?' a lover asked me years later, suspicion in her eyes.

'Yes.'

'Then where did it go? Did it fly away?'

'Yes. It flew away.'

'Wah! It had wings?'

'Yes. It had wings.'

'And it flew away overnight?'

I didn't answer. Not overnight, but little by little, year by year, quietly. Once, someone brought back three books with Uncle's name on them from the scrap market, 'Here, take them. Consider them your own!'

'So,' my lover said, shrugging as if a point had been proved, 'there was no library. Just the room where poor Chachcho slept alone.'

I remained silent.

'And Lalna and Uncle, together.'

'Right,' I said, tonelessly.

'Even the kids saw it from the skylight!' she snapped.

'So did I,' I told her.

'So who slept with whom?'

'Uncle…'

'…?'

'With me.'

'In the flying library?'

'No. In the sitting room by the boundary wall.'

'And in the big room?'

'Chachcho. With Lalna.'

❖

Lalna.

That was not her name.

What her name was, no one knew.

When I asked her, having overheard the furtive whispers of people, Lalna, who was standing on a stool wiping the ceiling fan with a wet rag tied to a stick, shook so badly that it seemed she would fall, taking me and Chachcho down with her, along with the stool and the table upon which it stood and which we were trying to hold steady. 'Who told you? Who? It must have been that Paresh. Didn't I tell you to stay away from his sort? Behen-ji, why don't you stop him? The boy will be spoilt. Don't shake the stool!' And she twirled the stick with the wet rag and hurled it at the floor, as if wanting to wipe not the dust off the fan but the curiosity off my face.

But her name wasn't Lalna.

What it was, no one knew. All they knew was that she had come crying one day to Premanand-ji's house, and from then on people knew her as Lallan's bahu.

But she wasn't Lallan's bahu. At least not in the usual sense of 'bahu'. She wasn't Lallan's daughter-in-law – she was his wife.

'How is it possible that no one knew who Lallan was?' the same lover asked me behind the tank on the roof. 'Here, they create people out of thin air. And you're telling me that a whole, hale human being disappeared?'

But behind the tank on the roof, words echo differently. The words remain the same, but their meanings change. No one knows... that you and I are here... that we have disappeared... from everyone's sight... Oh ho... Ai hai!

'Hale? Not at all,' I said in a different sort of haste, caressing my lover's neck.

'Was he mad?'

'Yes, yes, mad!' I panted.

But I didn't know that. Chachcho said that Lalna had told her.

But Chachcho said that Lalna had also told her that Lallan was dead and that Lallan's father had tried to force her into prostitution, which was why she ran away.

'Ran away? Bah!' my lover said. 'I heard that her father-in-law brought her here. She came wailing, and fell at her father-in-law's feet saying, don't do this bappa, don't leave me here bappa, your bahu will die bappa, and her nose started running as she cried and her father-in-law said, stay away, stay away, not to keep her hands away from his feet but to save his dhoti from her nose!'

Why did she have to start on all this – Lalna, Chachcho, Uncle – now, behind the tank, when all my actions were trying to tell her, let's talk about me and you! There's romance in the air, and there's you and me... This weather, this moment, just us and no one else... *Idhar main jawaan udhar tum haseen...* My youth, your beauty... The possibilities!

'Who knows,' my lover's eyes dropped as her imagination took flight, 'maybe it wasn't her father-in-law but Lallan himself who brought her here, to get rid of her so that he could go back to his new, second bride?'

'Yes... she... also... told us... that,' I said breathlessly.

'That Lallan brought her here?' Her eyes grew wide.

'No. That she was sick of his second wife so she ran away. But enough of that!' I scolded.

Who knows where she had come from? All we knew was this: someone had come to leave her and she'd cried and sniffled at his feet, but in the end, people said that Lalna had run away. Run away from Lallan, whom no one knew, not even where he was from. They didn't even care whether he existed or not. All they were interested in was Lalna – the magnet to which all their curiosity had attached itself.

Lallan's bahu, whom Uncle called 'Lallan ki' and Chachcho called 'Lalna'.

A kind of bitterness wells up inside me. Why did she have to come back now, when everything reminds me of Chachcho? As if she were some relic of hers, shadowing her every memory.

❖

I suspected nothing when I heard the doorbell ring.

I wasn't even startled. I just glanced at the telephone once and got up to open the door. A heap of moth wings on the ground stirred and settled down again.

I just stood there, realizing that this was all I had ever been doing – opening the door and finding Lalna in front of me. That action, of the parting of the two planks of wood, seemed to happen again and again in my life with the ceaselessness of slow motion. I keep opening the door in slow motion. I keep finding Lalna standing there.

Lalna came in. And then, silently, I followed her into the house.

Seeing a sheet – crumpled, almost like a turban – on the dining table, she stopped short.

It must have set, I muttered. Unfolding the turban revealed an earthen bowl. I noticed that when I'd kept the milk there at night, it had seemed lighter. Now, when I picked up the curd, it was heavy.

What I didn't notice was that my days of setting curd were at an end.

If I had, I wouldn't have pulled Chachcho's chair to Chachcho's window for Lalna to sit on. Lalna fell into it and I stood at the window, looking out.

Silence.

Which was not silence at all, but more like the threat of a storm about to gather and strike outside.

I said to Lalna, I told Chachcho, hey, it's one thirty, I looked at the watch, you're still awake?

I said, Chachcho stayed silent and just turned her eyes towards me once.

I said, I told her, it's very late, you should sleep.

I said tonelessly, Chachcho said, yes it's late now, I'll sleep. Lalna broke into sobs as if Chachcho had meant she was going to sleep forever.

I said, I turned off the light and went, as if I meant I had turned off the light of her life.

'If only I had been there...' Lalna came and stood beside me, as if she could turn on the switch I had turned off, as if such a switch existed.

In that moment of reliving Chachcho's death, though, I had forgotten all recriminations. There was only this – we were standing at Chachcho's window, in memory of Chachcho. Memory, from which particulars had slowly slipped away, leaving behind only a formless presence.

Extinguishing a match, I threw it out, as if there was nothing else to remember. Lalna took drags from my cigarette, as if there was nothing to forget.

Late into the night, she kept pacing around Chachcho's room. Climbing a stool to rehook a curtain that had come loose, slamming the door swollen from the rains again and again, taking Chachcho's books off the shelf, dusting them and putting them back in order of height, and finally standing at the window. At the same place where Chachcho used to stand.

Yes, I'll eat now, she said when I told her it was getting late and she should eat.

I didn't know then that these would be the last tender words I would say to her. That I would, once again, in anger, stop speaking to her.

But they were not her last words to me when she said, 'The key to Chachcho's Godrej?'

I saw little then, more later as I remembered, that she took out everything that had belonged to Chachcho – her most private things, her clothes, her expensive saris – and placed them on the bed, wiped the cupboard with a wet cloth, dried it, laid out fresh newspapers on each rack, and then opened everything, unfolded all the clothes, dusted them, wiped them, packed and folded them, and kept them back in the cupboard.

Serving Chachcho's memory? Or her own future?

❖

Now, I have to ring the doorbell when I come back from work.

When I rang it the first day, the door creaked open and I found Lalna standing on the other side. She was inside, I was outside.

Did I blink and stare at her, thinking that this act – of the parting of the two planks of the closed door, of her being on one side, of me being on the other – which had happened so many times before, was happening again?

Or did I think that we had changed places that day?

Or maybe I immediately stepped inside, but kept seeing

in my heart the perpetual opening of the door. Going to the stairs, past the porch, my feet suddenly stopped. Maybe because the smells, of jeera and hing being fried in desi ghee, wafting out of the kitchen reached me only then. As if the realization dawned only then that something was piercing the air that I had, in all these days, allowed to become still and stagnant in this house, like a shroud wrapped around me.

She has come again, to deprive me of Chachcho's love.

Frightened, I changed direction and started going upstairs, on tiptoe.

The way Chachcho must have, once.

And at the door at the top of the stairs, her heart must have skipped, her legs must have trembled. The roof beyond that door, not a roof but a sea, whispering, 'Come, come.' A call that had pulled Chachcho this far, but the fear in her still making her want to run back.

Not a roof but a sea that lay above Laburnum House. And not lay, but rolled. On Laburnum House, which wasn't one house, but a neighbourhood of a hundred or so houses that existed in one huge building stretching far and wide, that lay drowning for centuries under the rolling, sea-like roof that was high in some places, and in some places low.

Uncle could never understand. Why the quiet Chachcho, the Chachcho who would shrivel up if he so much as gave her a stern look, would sometimes suddenly sit up. What thought rose in her heart and flew up and away before she could catch it, leaving her more restless than ever, so that her feet would start, of their own accord, towards the stairs, as if someone had nudged her with an elbow: Wake up, you can't sleep. No, I can't sleep. Me neither. Then let's go. Go where? To the roof!

Chachcho stands at the top of the stairs, before the open door.

The last days of rain. The roof spreading far and wide. Its damp, musical magic. Its gentle rolling. Rolling and raising its musical arms. Raising its arms and gently tugging at the sky and stars. Their light swimming into her eyes.

When the roof is beneath your feet, there's the whole sky above.

We have started walking – me and my memory of Chachcho.

The flesh of Chachcho's arms hasn't started turning into water yet, so we will have to walk stealthily, away from staring eyes, making our way through the darkness. Chachcho bumps into her own arm and frightens herself.

Wherever the level of the roof changes, we have to go up or down a couple of steps. Or climb up a water tank and jump. Or leap from a ledge. Then Chachcho will have to gather her sari above her ankles.

Which she does.

She looks around. In a faraway corner, servants have laid out their masters' beds. The bright shadows of darkness.

When Chachcho's sari flutters in the breeze, she gathers it around her knees and easily climbs up the parapet. Then, as if walking a tightrope, she walks across and jumps down to the other side.

She, and I with her.

We keep walking, far away. Over countless houses, leaping over their suffocating walls.

At the end of the mohalla, I stop – one more step, and down!

At that moment, I feel her behind me. How long must she have been following Chachcho and me to have come this far?

I don't want to, but I have to turn back, and my memory of Chachcho is left behind, as if it has jumped over.

On the roof, the evening lights have started coming on, as if it is their secret desire to stay up all night and gossip with the darkness.

Lalna's hair is red.

Chachcho used to henna it for her with a brush.

Lalna started greying earlier.

But it was Chachcho who died first.

❖

I did not want some stranger to prepare Chachcho for the pyre.

You can't do it, son – the pundits, the elders, they all were adamant. It wasn't the time for arguments, so I stayed silent. How could I make them understand that, just because she couldn't say anything any more, it didn't mean that some stranger could see her body?

As she grew older, Chachcho covered up more and more of her body. A blouse cut like a kurti to cover her midriff. Long, loose sleeves, coming down to her fingers. The pallu covering her head, down to her forehead. Her face wrapped tight in her aanchal. Her feet covered in shoes or lost under her sari.

Uncle's death has broken her, the people airing themselves on the roof said. That's how devoted our women are.

No one thought that she might be covering up her aging beauty, erasing her shrivelling body from her own sight.

I'll change the large mirror in your bathroom, it has become clouded and stained with water, I had said. Let it be, she had replied, its flaws hide mine.

In my dumb heart, it is as if I see her reflection in the mirror, floating like a dream in the steam-filled bathroom.

Whenever I feel like crying, it's as if something big and restless in my chest starts panting. Not one tear comes out.

Chachcho...

Chachcho... What can I do, besides speaking your name?

Chachcho, Chachcho... Memories rustling like dry leaves. Memories like a magic lantern, moving from here to there in a flash, turning upside down, inside out, playing tricks.

This isn't right, I think. This memory, at least, must come soft and slow. This high speed, discotheque-style flashing doesn't suit it. This memory is my grief. Grief is slow, is deep, is seeping in, drop by drop. I think, I'm really sad, very sad, very, very sad.

I'm stuck in my sadness, and it drags me along, to memories – old, useless, endless.

I peep in from the skylight to where Chachcho's room used to be, but I can't make out much, except something just out of sight, some dream carefully folded and kept away.

It's because of my sadness that I have started dreaming in broad daylight. A dream not of the future, but of the past. Again, that tired old man, and memories of the past, bloodying him.

Even the happy moments from this world of memories give the old man more grief. Dreams that go backwards, not forward, can do nothing else. Like that heavenly beauty from childhood tales who turned out to be a witch when you noticed that her feet were turned backwards.

I return stealthily. To be alone. To remember Chachcho alone.

How meaningless these things are. To remember someone

dear, their death, a son crying for his mother – what is there to tell? I love Chachcho – what do these words mean?

I turned away immediately after lighting her pyre, I had no wish to see the fire blaze.

Is that how easy separation is? Lay her down, touch her with a flame, turn away. I came back home feeling utterly light and empty.

When I said namaste to bid the neighbours farewell, I felt as if the torch with which I had touched Chachcho one last time was still in my hand. I tucked it into my kurta and went inside. Inside my home.

Where there was no one.

Now there is. Once more. Lalna. Who came here when she heard the news, to pay her respects. The memory of her friend pulled her back here.

And the memory of her Bitwa.

❖

The sun's red rays come through the window and fall straight on my face. Bringing with them hints of the skull-cracking heat that comes after the rains. But I don't feel like getting up. I cover my eyes with the pillow, as if I can create the illusion that it's still night and go back to sleep again.

Lalna was used to sleeping with two pillows, but she didn't rest her head on even one. She would just make a two-inch tunnel between them, to burrow her head in.

Lalna, again! My first thought in the morning – Lalna!

Some people, even if they lie quietly in a corner, can spread everywhere like grief.

How strange – I'm mourning Chachcho, but it's Lalna who roams around here like a ghost.

Scared, I double up the sheet over my closed eyes so that I can't see that, wherever I look, Chachcho isn't there. Chachcho isn't around, not here, not there – the realization rumbles through my bed.

The door creaks open, then closes.

The creak, laboured in its attempt to seem effortless. It is Lalna's way of showing me that she has, quietly, without making a sound, checked on me, while taking every care to not disturb me.

It will creak again now.

With such deviousness, she waits for me.

Why does she wait? Can't she see that I take my cup of tea and head to wherever she isn't? I've even stopped sitting silently with her.

She can't summon the courage to say, wake up Bitwa, look how high the sun's risen! That is why the creak, the laboured attempt at effortlessness.

The imagined call of 'Bitwa' in her voice sends shivers down my spine.

Creaaak!

'What is it?' my pillow asks, at last.

'Should I make tea?' Lalna's voice replies.

Not Chachcho's.

Did I get up and come away because I hadn't yet heard Chachcho's voice? Because she hadn't brought me tea? I can't remember. Did I understand immediately, when I saw her sleeping in the chair?

At the window, the pigeons fluttered and flew. Had they been near Chachcho all night? Had they cooed and flapped all night, and had Chachcho been unable to lift even a finger to chase them away?

If the breeze from a flying pigeon's wings touches you,

you grow up healthy – that's what we used to say as kids on the roof.

'Should I keep the tea here?'

Lalna. Again. When she could have, if she wanted to, kept it without a word. I would have understood from the sound of the teapoy being moved.

I have to move the pillows off my face. My eyes don't go to her face but flutter nearby. Even so, I can see her mouth, which she is opening and closing for some reason, a thread of saliva forming and breaking between her teeth.

Did Chachcho, in her last moments, really want to call her, or did I just imagine it, seeing the shape of her half open lips? How I wish that thought hadn't occurred to me, and I hadn't gone and sent that telegram in the end – Lalna, Chachcho has died. My weary voice circles round and round inside me.

Lalna has brought out Chachcho's biscuit box. She stands, holding it open for me. Why is she trying to become Chachcho?

Chachcho. I try to open my mouth and say, 'Chachcho.'

Lalna. My lips form 'Lalna'.

When I pick up a biscuit, trembling in anger, a very civil 'thank you' comes out of my mouth.

Lalna looks at me intently.

When will you leave, I want to ask, moving my hands animatedly. Chachcho is gone, I want to remind her, how long will you stay to mourn?

You, I curse silently, are driving Chachcho away by staying here.

What is your programme? I think, with this question, I can touch upon the subject of her departure.

But two things happen. The word 'programme' reminds

me of a code the two of them had shared. And then I see that
Lalna is wearing Chachcho's sari.

❖

But did I say anything? It was a holiday, so I had a leisurely
bath and lay vacantly in bed. Then, a warning rang out in my
heart – the wall clock was showing 12:56.

I got up noisily, intending to reach the dining table before
the clock struck one, serve myself the food, and eat before
Lalna had the chance to say anything to me. The daal will be
tempered with chilli and garlic, the raita will have roasted
jeera, the kheer will have chironji seeds…

Have you come here to indulge my tastes, I'll ask, I think
as I lean at the basin to wash my hands. And keeping all
traces of rudeness out of my voice, I'll say, now you can go
and… As I splash my face with a palmful of water, I forget
the rest of the line – which I had only just come up with!

This is what's happening to me – one moment here,
another there, and no consciousness of anything. And just
you see, there won't be a plate at the table so that I'll have to
call her, and she will come and stand there with the plate and
then I will have to see her again, hear her again, as her eyes
brim over with affection.

The food is kept in a thermoseal container. Even the
plate is out! Underneath the glass, a note – 'I'll return in the
evening.'

When I uncover the daal, I let the fragrance of the lavish
spices steam warmly upon my skin. The relief of being alone.

I feel like going to Chachcho's room, which remains hers
even though she's gone.

But as I open the door I think – am I a thief? And this

Lalna has set up camp in my Chachcho's room. Like a needle pricking my memory of Chachcho, undoing stitches here, making new ones there…

I look at the things on Chachcho's table. A shell-shaped ashtray, filled with ash from Lalna's cigarettes, which I pick up and empty into the trashcan. A brass statue of baby Krishna sucking his toe. I used to strike the same pose, Chachcho would tell me.

And Lalna too, I just have to recall.

A fat copy of *Chandrakanta Santati* that Lalna had gifted Chachcho. Her handwriting in violet ink – 'For Chachcho'. Chachcho's name. Written by Lalna.

I touch the ashtray, open the book and caress Chachcho's violet name, and place Krishna on one side, the way Chachcho used to.

I glance towards the window, my gaze attracted by a fluttering butterfly. A blue butterfly that has flown in and is now sitting on the windowsill, where, many times every day, Chachcho would come and stand. A bit lost, looking absently outside, her languid eyes searching not for the road to Laburnum House, but for some imaginary one.

It's not blue, it's white. With two blue stripes on the white. When it flies it's blue, when it sits it's white.

When Chachcho flew away, did she turn the colour of her sari's border?

I think of Chachcho, but I keep seeing Lalna draped in her sari.

Get rid of her, I say to myself. I live with Chachcho, I remind myself. And I am living, moment by painful moment, with Chachcho's death.

If you've been a part of someone's life, you'll be a part of their death too.

But are you? Am I? Am I included at all in Chachcho's death?

Or is it just her, whose name was on Chachcho's lips in her last moments?

Whose name was it? Was it really Lalna's?

Whose room is this? Is it really Chachcho's?

I am completely, completely alone.

❖

Completely, completely alone.

I stand at the window where Chachcho used to stand. Alone. Not with me.

On the windowpane, her beautiful image comes alive. Looking at herself, along with the people coming to and going from Laburnum House. Her big eyes and delicate nose, as if made with the sharp tip of a pencil. Her full, purple lips. A deep purple, like the colour of jamuns.

'Uff!' Lalna would say. 'Just cut her open and see, this Chachcho doesn't have blood running through her veins, but the juice of jamuns!'

In the window, Chachcho lazily raises a hand and slowly undoes the ribbon in her hair, setting her curls free so that they cast a shadow over everything like dense clouds. She stands, wearing a gold-bordered sari – pink, green or sometimes sky blue – the pallu opening out like a Japanese fan under her left shoulder, and nearly slipping down the Maggie sleeve of her blouse that fits tight over her breasts.

She would rest her full, plump arms upon the windowsill. Like this.

'Uff!' Lalna would say. 'Enchantress, witch! Do you fill them up with a bicycle pump, these full, tight arms of yours?'

Chachcho would stretch languidly and cross her arms behind her head, the pallu slipping off her body and the cloth over her armpits dampening with sweat.

I've heard, I've heard, these things I've heard – from the people of the mohalla, from Chachcho herself, from Lalna too in some childhood of mine. The tellers telling it in such a way that I can see it now, as if I were there then, before me, after me! Looking at Chachcho who would stand here silently, as if made not of skin and bone, but of a melody. An invisible melody that gave her body the cascading beauty of waves.

That wave couldn't be hidden. Even when, later, she started covering herself up. It turned her thick, rough clothes transparent.

That wave was still in her when she sat on the chair in which she fell asleep forever. A wave that did not stop swirling even after her death. Her neck lolling below the armrest, her hand held away, her eyes following her hand, then turning upwards, her lips slightly open as if they were about to call someone – in that entire pose, the same rhythm, as if it were a mudra from a dance.

It wouldn't have been surprising if she had risen again and stood at the window!

The way I have been standing ever since.

Like a perfect painting, she'd stand and watch – What's that movement outside?

A three-wheeler is coming in through the gate, making gravelly noises on the path, raising dust with its wheels.

I step back, like Chachcho used to, shielding herself from the dust and from strangers' eyes. I close my eyes, as if no one will be able to see me if I can't see them. The very next moment, I open my eyes. Slightly curious, I stick my head out – who's in the rickshaw?

This curiosity isn't mine but Chachcho's.

How long will I remember to stay in the shadows? Will I not show myself? Rising like the sun from a corner of the window. A purple sun. Her bewildered eyes forgetting that someone is staring in from outdoors. Or becoming carefree with a toss of her curly locks – Let them look! Or turning those staring eyes into a mirror of her beauty, of her desire.

Slowly I start loosening my body, untying knots and undoing screws here and there. All the veins, all the sinews stretched, relaxed, and in this window, on an invisible point where the inside and the outside meet, I swing. Like a vine.

Like Chachcho.

My hands, here, my hair, there, the window my frame, and me, a beautiful picture in it…

The past, like a picture…

Sadness, like a picture…

She looks outside. I smoke a cigarette.

❖

The house opposite, where the maid is washing dishes – that used to be Premanand-ji's house. From where a girl, fifteen or sixteen years old, used to watch. There she is again, the woman in the window. Tussar sari, gold border. Silent, lost. Now she'll undo her ribbon and toss her curly hair. A big, round bindi on her forehead.

'Sulking, with her face puffed up like a pumpkin,' Lalna would nudge Chachcho with an elbow and tell me.

'I'd wish that she'd look my way so that I could make faces and tease her,' Lalna chirped. 'How long can someone keep sulking?'

'One day, as I was combing my hair, I noticed that some

girl in Premanand-ji's courtyard had stopped hanging out clothes to dry and started aping me.' Chachcho smiled softly. 'If I scratched my nose, she'd do the same. If I hissed and straightened out a snarl in my hair, she'd do the same. When I stopped moving my hands and started staring, she did the same.'

'Like this! And this! And this!' Lalna danced.

'Hey, you're very rude!' Chachcho withdrew from the window.

At that time, the skylight to Premanand-ji's house had become especially popular on the rooftop of Laburnum House. The girls of the mohalla would bring stories of a new girl who kept scolding the cook, and who, after having served food to Premanand-ji's entire household and having had them wash their hands, would drag a stool from a corner and sit to eat at that very table.

A new maid, a lot of people said.

'Some poor, distant relative,' Uncle gave Chachcho the news.

'Hey, shhh!' Chachcho cautioned, with a finger on her lips, when she saw Premanand-ji come out and head towards the courtyard.

'Hey, shhh!' the girl quickly aped and went back to wringing the clothes.

Chachcho started enjoying these games. When Uncle went out, she'd come to the window as usual, but now she was always glancing at the courtyard. She started waiting for the girl as if to see how far her own courage would take her – the proof of that courage being the girl who had become her mirror.

Chachcho started striking pose after pose, and seeing them repeated, she began to smile, as if falling in love with her own mischievousness. Sometimes she would lean as far out the window as she could and spread her arms as if they were wings, as if this bird would fly away. In the courtyard, the girl, too, started flapping her arms.

And, of course, it turned into a contest of who could go further. If one twirled, the other twirled faster, if one tossed her hips, the other tossed harder.

Startled, Lalna started laughing. Had she ever expected this close-lipped girl to start dancing!

Chachcho's heart started beating madly. Frightened by how her mind and body had started dancing. Sensing this, Lalna thumbed her nose at Chachcho, who also raised her hand, not to tease Lalna more but to make a friendly gesture..

People didn't see this happening. They were busy looking down skylights. The boys would say, it's great fun at night. They'd say that the new girl purposely slept right across from the door to the courtyard so that whenever Premanand-ji's nephew needed to go to the bathroom, he'd have to go past her. That when the bathroom light went on, you could see her from the skylight, asleep, wearing a torn skirt that had gathered above her knees, and Paresh told me that, by god, he'd heard from trustworthy sources that she wore nothing underneath.

There, in the courtyard, a dying yellow bulb hung on a naked wire. In its darkness, the courtyard was full of shadows. It was there that Chachcho slapped Premanand-ji's nephew.

'What did you say when you went into the courtyard?' I asked her once, lying beside her.

'What could I have said?' Chachcho replied, and switched the table fan to full speed.

❖

The table fan.

The same one that a thief had once tried to steal – while it was still running – by dropping down a rope from the roof to the courtyard, as if fishing in a pond! It was only after that, that either Uncle or Lalna or Chachcho got the courtyard covered with a trellis.

Summer nights!

And what does one do on summer nights?

One sleeps on the roof.

But the roof belongs to the whole mohalla, crowded and rushed, raucous and noisy, sneaking and peeking like the moon. Stealthy caresses. Mischief, like the wind. On a parapet somewhere, a clay jar is kept so that one can wake up at night and drink water, fragrant with damp earth, from it. Sheets have been spread out on beds, pillows have been rolled into bolsters, laughter fills the air. At a distance, someone has a brazier going and is taking dough from a platter and rolling it to make hot chapattis. A squirrel has woken up, hopeful of getting at the dough, taking two frightened steps forward, then taking twenty back, twice as scared.

The roof of Laburnum House. Sometimes still called the bankers' roof. In the 18th century, this used to be a mohalla of bankers, and their king made this place for them to live and earn their livelihood, all under one roof. A roof that went high and low. A roof of wonders for all seasons. A roof that fostered all relations. A roof free from all pressures. A roof leaping from infinity to infinity.

Who knows how many rebels this roof sheltered in 1857, and when a troop of British soldiers came looking, they must have run over the roof, from house to house, and jumped down into the mohalla and disappeared! It's said that among Chaman-ji's forefathers were two brothers, one of whom sided with the rebels and the other with the British, and in those days of slaughter, they'd give shelter to their people, hidden from each other. One day, one of the hidden people from one side was running away, via the roof, while another from the other side was coming in to hide, via the same route. They both crashed into each other, fell from a higher level of the roof to a lower one, and one of them sprained his leg. The other pulled him over the parapet before disappearing.

It's easy to disappear on this roof even today. Someone's home has two storeys, another's has three, somewhere there's a staircase from the porch, somewhere an iron ladder against the wall by the courtyard. On the roof, overgrown trees, overhanging branches, poles, parapets, water tanks. A step here, a step there, and gone!

Knowing all this, Sudhirchandra ran in 1942 when the police came to catch his father who was active in the freedom struggle. Run my child, run, his grandmother screamed, your father isn't here so these killers will shoot you instead! Then she started cursing them: traitors, uniform-wearers, mules of the British!

The funny thing is that Sudhirchandra, though not a traitor, wasn't much of a patriot either. He was doing his Inter or BA at the time and just wanted to get a good job somewhere, working for black or white or yellow or red – it didn't matter. He only ran so that his troublemaker of a father wouldn't ruin his prospects. But this time, there was nobody to lend a helping hand, or to move aside. On one side, there was the branch of a neem tree, on the other, the policeman's moustache! They say that Sudhirchandra was about to leap onto the branch and hang on for dear life when he heard his grandmother screaming, 'Arey, you'll die,' almost dying herself from climbing the stairs, her walking stick going rata-tat. Sudhirchandra hesitated, and ended up so neatly in the policeman's arms as if that was what he had intended to do all along! He was taken to the police station and a report was filed, 'Let him go,' the policeman said – Sudhirchandra told us, twirling a non-existent moustache – and he was let go, but was officially declared a freedom fighter. And this is how he got grace marks in the provincial judicial examination. See, he said, my grandmother made me an officer.

Knowing all these stories about the roof, the fan-thief decided to try his luck.

'I thought, why has the fan started rocking?' Chachcho would recall.

'Thief! Thief! I shouted,' Lalna would add. 'I got up intending to pull at the rope and bring the rascal tumbling down, but your Chachcho was more concerned about the sheet for we had thrown off our pallus and opened up our blouses in the heat!'

On hearing the cry of thief-thief, the people on the roof started running helter-skelter. Many would claim: I almost caught him, but he slipped away. Someone said he was tall and strong, had oiled his body and wore only a loincloth. Someone else said he was short and monkey-like, and leapt into the darkness. He had a dagger, a third said.

Many said nothing. Amidst the stampede, they busied themselves with furtive kisses.

When Uncle and I went towards the courtyard, Lalna and Chachcho were snatching at the same sheet, trying to cover themselves, here a blouse was being pulled on, there a dhoti was being tucked.

And in the moonlight, all at once, many glistening breasts.

❖

When someone departs, leaving behind only this roof and its skylights, it's as if a melody starts rising like a gathering storm. All kinds of happy and sad moments, from here and there, yesterday and today, fly in and merge with it to now tell the story that could not be told then.

Chachcho, who was not my mother, my anguish over that fact hurting me more and more since my childhood. Whom I consider in every way, in every condition, my mother. If you were there, I'd tell you all this, Chachcho, my mother – you, no one else.

Is it so, that we see those who were there only when they are no longer there?

Is it so, that we only live what's not there, and the things that are there remain mere mechanical habits until they recede into dreams?

For example, if I say – which I don't want to because I don't want to talk about all that – that I am, now, more of this house, this roof and my childhood than I ever was then, when in my youth and childhood I could be seen enjoying myself in this house and on this roof, because then I was lost in the dreams of a foreign land, dreams that the residents of this mohalla had forced upon me by telling me that, being born in Hong Kong, I had a British passport because Hong Kong had, then, still not found freedom. I was only a fun-loving child puffed up with the air of unbelonging, who could be seen here but was actually already there, where I would supposedly go. The losses here were no losses, the victories here were just time-pass.

A young man at Laburnum House once made us kids race across the roof, with the promise that he'd allow the top ten to play with the iron muscles of his arms and chest and would let them swing in pairs from his arms which he held crossed behind his head and turned into a ride as he twirled around like a whirling top! All the kids ran with all their might at the shout of ready-steady-go and, one by one, they left me behind.

How difficult can it be to be one among ten? Even I ran.

Seeing the crowd running ahead of me, I must have faltered. Slowly, I must have turned to see how many remained behind me.

Just the lone Paresh in the distance, loping towards me! I turned and ran to him.

We both must have laughed. He must have said they're all frogs. I must have thought, never mind this race here, the only race that matters is the one there, where I will belong because I was born in Hong Kong, just let me do some more time-pass and grow older!

The life that is, is unreal – the life that will or might be is real!

I'm not laughing at myself, I'm crying at the injustice of the wrong womb bearing me, and the many marvellous birth-rights it separated me from. No one says it, yet the echo still falls in my ears, that this is how it was, that Lalna's stomach kept growing for nine months, and then no one knows how or when a child 'arrived' from Hong Kong and started living with this family. That child, whose mother is Chachcho not Lalna, my heart says, or wants to say.

Then, again, I start recalling my old life, my rooftop childhood, which was false but believable and fun because I had with me, in my heart, a football – my real future in a foreign land – and every little thing made it bounce higher and higher.

We didn't touch it, it was the roof perhaps that kicked our dreams up high with a kick of love. The branches of the trees

would hug the roof and the leaves would jump with joy –
why hang on the trees when we can tumble along with the
dreams on the rooftop! The whole sky would reach down
and join in their games.

When you are standing on the roof, with the tall trees
behind you and the sky above, then your childhood too will,
pushing real and unreal aside, march ahead, like a dream,
with nothing to stop it.

❖

With the sky above and the roof under your feet, what fetters
can't you unfetter? Had Ghalib not been living amidst the
rooftops of Delhi and Agra, he couldn't have said, *ishq par
zor nahin* – there's no way to restrain passion. And where
then would the grannies warm their bones on cold winter
afternoons? Where would the cow-dung hearths for cooking
baati go? Where would the burning sand be in which the
bharbhuja roasted bajra stems, beans and peapods, while
groups of children stood watching respectfully, in wonder,
as if the secrets of the universe were being revealed, the
warm wafting fragrance revealing them even more, and no
child would jump around, but instead stand quietly, poems
forming in her head that she would write years later.

Such was the magic of the rooftop that before the boys
of Laburnum House could sprout hair in their armpits, they
would develop an interest in the geography of a woman's
body. When some middle-aged aunt lying nearby on the
roof asked them to massage her legs, they would gingerly
walk over her overturned body, clutching her walking-stick,
wanting to measure the depths of the crevice between those
female buttocks. When my friend Paresh tried to measure

Sumi Aunty with his foot, he got a solid thrashing and found himself straight in his father's court. Afterwards, all of us on the roof would repeat his father's mantra to tease him. 'Son, remember: Money goes, nothing goes. Health goes, something goes. Character goes, everything goes.'

But only idiots didn't know that on the roof, anything and everything goes. Low or high, without distinction or discrimination, her husband or his wife, everything goes.

Meaning, anything could happen!

Is the roof made of candy, Uncle told me to ask them, and I naïvely did, without naming him.

'Sun and shadow,' Lalna said, 'in the day.'

'Light and dark,' Chachcho said, 'in the night.'

All possibilities existed within those lines.

When the women and children and servants would crawl out like an army of ants from their holes below and gather on the roof, they would never want to stop. Snacks, titbits, more snacks, more titbits, and riding on these, the women's gossip, the clinking of their bangles, the lifting of their veils. The servants would have their own business, hanging wet clothes out to dry, lighting a beedi, chewing tobacco. On one side, the children's playfulness, the teenagers' wilfulness on the other.

The men, owners of homes, came up to the roof after work, the only ones with some reserve, with some sense of purpose. Sometimes, only to sleep at night. Not for them the restlessness of women, the indolence of servants, the childishness of children, or the sensual escapades of youth. Very well behaved. Sometimes, they'd look like they had stepped into a harem by mistake, where they were supposed to come only after the servants had put up an improvised curtain made of saris!

Uncle didn't find anything about the roof interesting either. If someone like me did find it interesting, he'd put it down to childishness. As for the rest – like Lalna – it could only be the sign of an unruly heart.

He'd tell Chachcho, don't go up there unnecessarily, it's a waste of time, and for days on end, he'd forget that she might be going up there unnecessarily.

Treat her just as a servant, nothing more, he said about Lalna, when he thought things were getting out of hand on the roof.

Lalna, whose disrepute was a provocation to Laburnum House. More so, because Lalna was quite the beauty.

❖

Not this one. Not this lumpy Lalna who spreads out like fermented dough wherever she sits.

She clears her throat outside my room.

In a little while, she'll clear her throat again.

It's not a cough. She's telling me something.

She's telling me: I am.

She's telling me, I am am am, I am! Telling me, see how much I respect your space, I won't come inside and potter around, or talk and disturb your work, your rest, your mourning. Telling me, see how much I respect you no matter what you're doing, useful or useless, I consider it your right and let you do it.

Also telling me, I know you are Chachcho's, not mine, still I remain humble, courteous.

I open the door with a jerk.

She looks at me and goes back to whatever she was doing, as if I'm the one disturbing her, as if she's the busy one! She's polishing Chachcho's Moradabad pots, saucers and other brass pieces with a lemon. On her nose is a slimy fibre from the lemon, and near it the mole which, aping Chachcho, I'd run to swat with a newspaper screaming, fly, fly!

The lemon has turned blue, and a sour smell rises from Chachcho's sari, which Lalna has been wearing regularly.

She had let me know some days earlier by announcing loudly to the maid that it's very hot, I thought it would rain and nylon would be good, but I can't take it any more, I need cotton, so I'm using Behen-ji's saris for now.

Saris.

Like so much else that I'm now past counting. I feel sad. Chachcho spoilt her by fanning the flames of her greed. After shopping for the household, Lalna only had to say – So much sweat! It's all right when you're sitting in a rickshaw, but the moment you get off all the creases are ruined, as if you haven't come out of a rickshaw but some pot you'd been curled up in! Such is cotton's ploy, she'd laugh at her own joke. Or at her ploy, which was better than cotton's. And Chachcho would immediately give her money to buy nylon and chiffon saris. Why are you forcing me to take this, you're very stubborn, Behen-ji, Lalna would say.

The helplessness of greed!

These people know how to ask without asking. They throw out a big fat hint and if you catch it and decide to give them something out of the goodness of your heart, are they to blame?

It's cold, she would say through chattering teeth, Behen-ji this shawl turned out to be too thin, the shopkeeper cheated me and now I've run out of money. And Chachcho would, one by one, bring out her jamavars, pashminas, phulkaris and wrap them around her saying, when do I wear them, where do I go that I need to wear them, he brings something new for me every time, I just need this one, it's very warm and goes with everything.

Chachcho with one black shawl, and Lalna with a new colour every day.

This does look good on me, but Behen-ji, why don't you try it on, it will look even better on you, yes, you're right, it makes the cheeks look pink, but why don't you try it on, don't just leave it for the rats to get at.

Any decent person would hand it over – better you than the rats!

Lalna never asked for anything. Instead, she only rescued things that had been left to rot. So we should be the ones thanking her!

She coughs again. I am, she's reminding me. I am spending all my efforts, my time, my life in taking care of you.

It's not a cough, it is a complaint: Alas, cruel life, how misunderstood I am!

Is she preparing for some great sacrifice – to forever become a part of my life by giving up hers for me?

A cough again.

This time from my throat.

It's not a cough. It's a cry of fear!

❖

Even Chachcho got a fright one day.

That girl – who, when she wasn't ironing clothes for Premanand-ji or his children, would be learning lessons from their old books – laughed and said: I didn't demand that you come to the roof to meet me. I was just crying in the courtyard. Can't I even cry when I feel like crying?

'One day, she wasn't aping me,' Chachcho said. 'She was just standing in the courtyard, crying.'

At first she felt like pulling a face to tease Lalna, but she wasn't even looking in her direction. Forgetting all mischief, forgetting their game of daring, forgetting herself – she was shedding tears.

'What happened?' Chachcho waved and tried to get Lalna's attention.

Lalna saw her, but pretended not to. As if all her attention was concentrated on scrubbing clothes with that long yellow bar of '501'detergent soap.

Chachcho was agitated. The girl's sobs rose from the soap bubbles like little barbs to hurt her.

'I was scared,' Chachcho said. 'Why was *this* girl crying so much?'

'I'll also cry,' she felt. As if the aping game had become a part of her.

'I must find out,' she suddenly thought when Lalna put the washed clothes in a bucket and starting heading upstairs.

Chachcho picked up a jar of pickle and also went to the roof.

The first programme!

'What happened... Did what... Tied walnuts in the pyjamas... that too, whole... Of course they'd be visible... Oh, his nephew... such ways, despite being married...'

Whisper whisper, murmur murmur.

The first programme.

Then the second. Then more. And then, there was no stopping.

There she stands, seventeen-year-old Chachcho, at the window, waiting for the chatterbox to come out. Dumb gestures aren't enough now. She craves words.

'Come out somehow, anyhow, you wretch!'

The sound of a door closing.

She's dragging Premanand-ji's grandson's tricycle.

The wheel gets stuck.

She reverses, frees it.

Walks on.

Carefully gets it down from the verandah to the courtyard.

Walks to the tap.

Places the cycle under the tap and opens it.

The water splashes.

Lalna jumps.

Rolls up the legs of her salwar.

Bends.

Two thick ponytails swing on either side.

Remembers something.

Looks up.

Her eyes find the window.

She sees Chachcho.

Laughs.

'Programme?'

'Programme!'

Their only source of joy.

Chachcho would sneak out and leave a note about the programme pressed under a brick. 'Midnight meal on the roof.'

Lalna would fire up a brazier. Chachcho would make little cuts in the eggplants and insert cloves of garlic into them. In a corner of the roof, the eggplants would roast, crackling.

'Look, how the poor thing's suffering,' Lalna would whisper as it cooked.

They'd mash it with green chillies and salt and oil, wrap it in chapattis and feed each other. Hidden among the dancing shadows of the roof.

❖

'Don't bore me,' Paresh said years later, punching me, 'with this talk of programmes.'

He knew other things.

For every programme in Laburnum House, rose a rumour that Lalna had been seen on the roof sneaking up to meet a man! Each time a new lover. Even Uncle was spotted once.

Advice flew around: Take care of your sons!

In the darkness, nothing was seen but everything was heard – A man asking, 'Here?' Lalna saying, 'Here's good.' The man saying, 'And here?' Lalna giggling, 'Here's good too.' The man's voice becoming more mischievous, 'And what about here?' 'Oh! That's enough,' Lalna complaining, 'don't let your hand go any further.' 'Then she screamed,' Paresh started panting, 'saying, "Hey, I'll hit you, let me go," and the man laughed and suddenly they both became very quiet.'

'Know why?' Paresh asked.

'Why?' I said.

'Think,' he said.

I thought, and stayed silent. When my friend seemed more interested in his own story, why would I stop him? It was enough that he was my friend and that, in his eyes, I wasn't tainted by Lalna's disrepute.

Some people are like that – I thought, but didn't tell Paresh – invisible even in plain sight. Lalna could come onto the roof openly and go past people and they wouldn't even notice. Where she was, they couldn't see her. And where she wasn't, they'd see her again and again!

'Why should I worry, then?' Lalna giggled. 'Even if I'm in my bed, sleeping, they'll say they saw me in someone's lap or embracing someone else. Then why shouldn't I do as I please?'

No one saw Chachcho. The good girl from a good family, the wife of a husband who worked in Hong Kong. She was peaceful, gentle, withdrawn, and could be nowhere but in her house at night, certainly not among those who were seen in the debauched darkness. If they couldn't even think it, how could they see it?

'Only the roof,' Chachcho would say.

'Our roof,' Lalna would say.

Which has spread itself beneath the two girls' feet, and wants to fill their hair with stars. The breeze fans them and they open their hair. When the roof churns the cloudy skies, countless stars rain down on them. They tell each other everything. Everything that girls tell each other.

No one sees the two of them, because they're seeing one with someone else and not seeing the other at all.

The girls take off their slippers. They walk on the roof barefoot. They hold hands and walk to the edge of the mohalla. The houses are far below and the masters and mistresses have been left far behind!

This is their world. They hold each other tight so that they don't fall down from an overdose of happiness in this free kingdom of theirs. The roof laughs and moves beneath their feet, scaring them a little.

'Hey, can we stay here till dawn?' Lalna says.

❖

That Lalna. Whom I was ready to associate with, in spite of the occasional embarrassment, because she was Chachcho's friend.

For a long time, children have no past. That's why, for a long time, other people with no past don't trouble them either. What you can see in front of you is the whole story.

But there's a story at the back too, where you don't look. It's also to the left, and also to the right. We're right in the middle and all around us is a story, and some of us can see this part, and some of us can see that part.

And what about the story inside us?

I don't want to tell! I want to keep that story hidden inside me. And the image hidden in that story, I want to bury. Forget him, that nephew of that uncle from Hong Kong who dreamed of growing older and, as soon as he was an adult, of flying in an airplane to that foreign land whose citizenship was his birth right.

It can't happen, because it's not true that being born in Hong Kong automatically makes you a British national. It was a joke that his uncle played on him, and that the people of Laburnum House, knowingly or unknowingly, let him dream about.

It also can't happen because he was born to a woman with an unspoken but sullied past.

But I don't want to say it, I don't want to reveal my secret. I want to be far away from that nephew whose vast dream towers over my failures. I want to return to my Chachcho's lap where no defeat can harm me.

I want to be enveloped by that womb which, in not giving birth to me, caused me such anguish.

'What is the matter?' she would ask, tenderly brushing the sweaty hair off my forehead.

Where did that hand go? To which world? Frozen in what gesture? Lightly leaning on that windowsill? With clipped nails that had been shaped with a file?

Two golden bangles?

And a safety pin swinging from them?

I smile. At the thought of being sadder about not being able to see that hand in its new surroundings than at Chachcho's passing.

That's why I return to the past again and again. Running from myself. Running from Lalna. To Chachcho, only Chachcho.

But what's the use of running? Both Lalna and I follow me everywhere. In my desperation to escape them, I end up turning my full attention to them. As a result, Chachcho lies forgotten!

Chachcho used to say that all of Laburnum House wanted to get rid of Lalna, even Premanand-ji. Yes, she's from his village, a distant relation, but then she should live like that, like a poor relative. Even if they don't call her a servant, she is one and should remain one. Why should she approach anyone with her head held high? Why lead our sons on by playing I Spy with them? Why wreak havoc on the roof by flinging her dupatta aside and taking her slippers off, going barefoot and bareheaded?

I wasn't there but Uncle was.

❖

When Uncle woke up early in the morning, the corners of his eyes would be filled with gunk.

'He was getting really spoilt, your Uncle,' Lalna would tell me. 'Like an untamed bull, without a mother or father. Did he want to marry or did he just want to rein himself in? And Chachcho, also without a mother or father, but a girl.'

'And then your Uncle found her, this glass of sweet falooda,' Lalna would say, pinching Chachcho.

Winter or summer, Uncle would go straight to the tap and splash water on his eyes for a long, long time.

Uncle had a reputation in Laburnum House. Hard-working, well-off, travelling regularly to Hong Kong, which was like having one foot in Britain. So what if it was the land of the Chinese – there were lots of white men too.

Then he would clear his throat so loudly as if it wasn't phlegm that he wanted to cough out, but his intestines.

Uncle's room always looked like the waiting room in a railway station, as if he was a traveller perpetually waiting for his train. Piles of saris wrapped in blue and pink polythene that the coolies would carry. His mug, soap, brush, tongue-cleaner and shaving implements drying on the bed, about to be packed into the trunk. The trunk itself lying open on the floor for his clothes to be folded and placed inside. His handkerchief and watch on the table to wear. Gathering everything else, he would be on his way.

After the throat clearing and the eye washing, Uncle would change out of his kurta and pyjama. Even at home he'd be packed and ready to get up and go. His trousers belted tight, his shirt buttons done all the way up to the collar, socks and shining shoes – all of this, even in the height of summer.

And when he opened a bottle of foreign liquor, he would put on his hat, which otherwise hung on a rack nearby.

He drank alone, and often he didn't even notice when Chachcho washed and ironed his shirts and came to keep them. 'Where have you been? Come here,' Uncle would say if he saw her. Chachcho would turn to go but he'd laugh and grab her arm.

'Why are you sitting like a sack of clothes,' he'd ask her and lift Chachcho as if she were a doll, not a sack of clothes, and set her up on a high divan so that her legs dangled in the air.

Then he would spread out more things across the already cluttered room. He would take out bars of soap and tubes of toothpaste from his trunk and make Chachcho smell them and drop them in her lap and all around her, as though he wanted to make a mountain out of them to bury Chachcho under. He'd unroll bolts of colourful nylon and dacron over her body and Chachcho would quietly let him do it, as if this hat-wearing, laughing creature were a sprung toy that would keep doing what it was programmed to until it finally wound down.

'Will you come... I'll take you to Hong Kong... then Indonesia... Fiji...' One after the other, Uncle would hand her dreams, like peacock feathers.

And Chachcho would hold on to them, curiosity lighting up her eyes as she looked, unbelieving, at the photographs Uncle showed her from foreign magazines, cuttings which he'd later put away like treasure in his trunk. 'Whaaa...' Chachcho managed to contain most of her wonder, but some still slipped out.

By morning, Uncle would forget all about it.

He also forgot Chachcho's slap.

That she had landed on his cheek one night when he went on like this with no sign of stopping. Chachcho threw the bottle to one side of the courtyard, then stood up, surprised by the sound of glass shattering. Uncle stood rooted with a hand on his cheek and then, pushing the mountain of things to one side of the bed, went off to sleep.

The next day he asked, 'Did you hit me last night?'

'No,' said Chachcho, and both of them stared at the shattered glass in the courtyard.

Then, putting on his socks and shoes, Uncle started packing.

And when in Hong Kong, was he always, similarly, all dressed and ready to return?

Maybe we just don't know how to live in one place. Maybe we're always preparing for a journey. And after that journey, for our life in that new land – where we'll start preparing for the next journey to the next destination.

Why do we always have to live in the future? I've come up to the roof again, as if it will reveal to me the new life that Chachcho came here thirsting for.

Some gazebos and pillars stand here in a philosophical manner, motionless, as if in deep thought. A monkey wanders into my field of vision. Sitting alone on top of a high gazebo, he makes the sky behind him appear sad.

Suddenly he jumps. As if into infinity.

My heart leaps. The monkey has disappeared, but that leap into infinity will remain forever etched in my memory.

❖

When I returned home, Lalna was telling the maid, it's still hot and humid, even though the rains have gone.

Having flung off her sari's aanchal, she was fanning herself, cardboard in hand, her fat arms jiggling. She was wearing a sleeveless blouse, sheer, red and with nothing underneath.

Both fell silent. I tried to avoid their gaze and went towards my room.

If she sees me, she stares as if there's nothing else to look at.

Then I turn frantically to Chachcho.

Even Chachcho's death wasn't this painful.

Sometimes pain turns into a dark, heavy blanket that wraps itself around you, and you fall into a strange, lifeless sleep. Pitch darkness, no sound, no movement, you even forget to feel sad – why should I not call it peace?

But what happens when someone comes to pull away that blanket, to tear it? That forgotten, lifeless sadness fights its way back into the light. Sometimes it quivers in the heat of the sun, sometimes the wind inflames it.

I run in search of some dark, safe place, forcing myself to remember Chachcho, forcing myself to forget the others.

As if they're somehow linked – my forgetting the others and my remembering her.

And is Chachcho becoming more dear to me, the more I'm irritated by the others?

I have to laugh at this grotesque thought. If I believe that I need to fill up my mind with Chachcho only in order to push Lalna out, I really should laugh at myself.

And isn't laughter a way of crying?

When I'm sitting alone, sometimes I feel like laughing loudly, freely, snorting, cackling. You think you've gone, Chachcho? You think you've moved on to another world where I can't reach you? Are you so foolish that you don't know where you are?

Here! Near me. With me.

I'm sitting, having dinner, and you don't even know that you're sitting across from me, looking at me?

Before I came along, you'd eat with your hands only when Uncle was in Hong Kong. Even if he was sleeping in the next room, you'd eat with a spoon.

'You don't stand at the window, do you?'

'No.'

A conversation between Uncle and Chachcho.

'On the roof…?'

'No.'

'Did you wake up at night…?'

'No.'

'But the bed was empty…?'

'No.'

But let it go – Uncle's no longer around. Relax. Eat with your hands, make slurping noises.

But Chachcho doesn't.

She isn't there.

The chair in front of me is empty.

I can sense steam forming inside me, slowly, very slowly. I close my eyes, focusing slowly on that steam. Slowly, very slowly, the steam is turning into a drop, I can feel it turning into a drop. The drop slowly rises and I know that it's rising. The drop will come up to the surface. I will not let it surface.

❖

The last month of the monsoon, but still no sign of rain. The air is sticky and humid, but the sun shines bright and hot.

Still, I come up to the roof, even during the day. It's so hot that the tar is melting and my body is burning. Sometimes I search for shade, sometimes I let the sunlight scorch me.

During the day especially, the roof looks different. People have started putting up boundaries to divide it. If nothing else, they line up potted plants to mark their territory. Instead of relaxing, they now sit belligerently in their separate homes, as if they've put up large signs on their faces – No Trespassing! And people outside the boundaries glare back with the same belligerence, as if to say – Leave? Why? We won't leave!

We weren't always like this. We would look down skylights, but we'd also respectfully step around the invisible boundaries of all sorts of people sitting in the open. We didn't have the need for physical boundaries then. Everyone knew that there would be couples under the jacaranda tree, that the municipal aluminium tanks were sites of romance; we'd live and let live.

Now people have their own separate plastic tanks. For water. Which are too small for romance. It's less a question of cover, than the right combination of shade and support.

Trees have been cut down too, so the leaves don't ring any more like little bells, the dance of light and shade no longer takes place.

Their branches have been replaced by TV antennae!

I keep wandering in this garden of antennae for a long time. Even broken ones have somehow been made to stand upright with coils of wire. When people have cut down on buying milk and fruit to buy TVs, of course they'll try to save their antennae till the very end!

Only servants come up to the roof in the harsh sunlight. The sound of scooters indicates a lot more coming and going taking place downstairs. Many women also drive nowadays.

When Lalna started driving Uncle's scooter, no one was happy except Chachcho. Even I couldn't help being angry when I saw her. She was making a mockery of us all.

My cheeks are burning. I stand on a tank from where I can see the road. Whenever a wedding procession went by, I used to run out. Chachcho too. Lalna would drag her out.

A car or horse decked with flowers. Where's the groom? Behind the flowers. His nose must be really big if it's poking out of the veil! What a gorgeous crown! Can you see his face? Where? What does he look like? There he is.

As if he was some movie star.

When the parade floats went past on Dussehra, Chachcho and I would run out.

Lalna too.

An election rally. Shouting over loudspeakers to ask for votes.

The Prime Minister's visit.

Houses would empty out. Everyone would go up to the roof and stand at its edges and corners in such a way, it seemed as if they'd mapped out the geography of Laburnum House. Like we'd make India on Republic Day at school, standing in our PT uniforms to form the country!

Children must have run out to watch when Chachcho's funeral procession went past too.

But not us. Not Chachcho and me.

Not even Lalna.

Poor thing, people must have said. She was so nice, they must have said. Her husband must have done something very good in his past life to have found such a forbearing wife, they've always said. Poor thing, they say again and again. See, how compassionately she let her husband's lover stay, even after becoming a widow. Poor widow's dead now, they must have said. Look, there goes a corpse, the children must have said.

But I can't connect Chachcho with that word. She was not *that* word.

I jump off the tank but keep walking around the roof for a long time, observing its contours, high and low. Until darkness descends upon the setting sun like a net, until it strangles the whole roof like grief. When there are no dreams left anywhere, just a black nothingness, I go back home.

Where I go, nowadays, like an escaped convict!

In the darkness, I hear someone whistling.

All the lights at home are switched off. Only the lamp in Chachcho's room casts a little light and a big shadow.

I stop dead in my tracks. The same scene once more – Chachcho in her chair, having fallen to one side. On the grill, pigeons the colour of darkness.

She is whistling.

But is she whistling?

But she is Lalna!

Hearing my footsteps, she freezes. The pigeons start flapping their wings.

'Corpse' – that word, which has been buried in my heart, surfaces.

As if someone else has said it!

❖

Lalna said that when she called out to Chachcho, everyone in Laburnum House ran to their doors and windows to look, as if they were all her Behen-ji!

'Call?' Chachcho chided Lalna. 'You think those screams that pierced the sky were calls?'

Uncle was in the toilet at the time. Even its door shook.

Lalna's screams had the same effect as the drums used to gather an audience at street corners before a tamasha. Uncle hurried and, holding up his pyjama with one hand, came to the window where Chachcho had already stationed herself.

In the verandah across from them, Premanand-ji was

alternately kicking Lalna like a football and hitting her with a stick like a hockey ball. And wherever Lalna fell screaming, the eyes of the gathered spectators followed.

Uncle forgot to tie the drawstrings of his pyjama.

How much more could a decent man like Premanand-ji bear, was the general opinion. She was determined to make a laughing-stock of him after all he'd done for her – he'd given her a place to eat and sleep, he even tried to make her study. It wasn't his nephew's fault at all, the whole world knew how this girl behaved. You could give her nice clothes to wear, but how could you change her nature?

Chachcho made no sound, but sometimes even when nothing is heard or seen, just a slight rustle in the air is enough for the world to find out. The whole crowd turned towards Chachcho's window.

Chachcho turned towards Uncle and, almost tearing through him, rushed upstairs.

Women forgot their excuses. Men and children were, of course, excused from excuses. Wiping their hands full of chutney, flour, ink, grease, oil, soap, whatever, on their clothes, everyone started rushing to the roof. How many smells must have risen with them all at once and mingled, if only for a moment.

As if this were the Ramleela of Ramnagar, where the stage kept shifting and people moved for miles together to keep up with it.

Not miles in Laburnum House, but from windows and skylights to roofs and parapets. Where the action shifted, there the crowd went.

They say everyone looked serious. Only one child broke the silence, gesturing towards Lalna. Not Lalna really, but the half-peeled banana in her hand. 'I want to eat,' he'd barely

opened his mouth when his mother gave him a tight slap
without taking her eyes off the tamasha, so that he stumbled
and fell and stayed down.

The crowd moved from this roof to that, Lalna rolled from
the verandah to the courtyard.

Chachcho opened the door at the top of the staircase and
was on the roof. She had come up barefoot. The crowd saw
her fly like an arrow. Onward and straight to the door from
which Lalna used to come up to meet her in secret. Chachcho
went down, and the crowd saw her slap Premanand-ji's
nephew and turn to Lalna.

They turned again to see the door of the roof through
which Chachcho was dragging Lalna like a stubborn mule.
When the half-peeled banana dropped from Lalna's hand,
the boy, who'd been sitting quietly all this while, stood up.

If Uncle had tied his drawstring, it's possible that that
moment wouldn't have been so anti-climactic. When he,
having run out from the toilet midway and more worried
about holding his pyjama up, couldn't raise his hand to push
Lalna away.

Did the slipping pyjama give Chachcho so much courage
that, later, whenever she had to stand up against Uncle she
would do so as firmly as she had done that day? She would
be like a strong gust of wind and Uncle would just swing
harmlessly away like a bit of rope. And Chachcho would
go past as if she had just cut through whatever had been
standing in her way.

❖

Go past – and, now, just gone. Not cutting through Uncle,
who wasn't there, not cutting through Lalna, who wasn't

there either, when she went away forever. Just me. And this time, Chachcho went away, cutting through me.

I stand rooted to where I was.

Not rooted but robbed, by Chachcho's death which pains me more and more every day.

And what was there to Chachcho's death? Nothing, nothing at all. I was less alone that day than on other days! Chachcho was lying near me on a slab of ice, wrapped in a white sheet and marigolds. From where I sat, her feet seemed to be blessing me. I could have, whenever I chose, removed the sheet and rubbed her body, blue from the cold, to give it once more the warmth of blood.

It was only because the people of Laburnum House had nothing better to do that they were talking about her.

Chachcho – her familiar image – remained even after her death.

Then why did she fly away like a wisp of cotton?

Immediately with the passing of that image, something happened. Every day other images, old and new, kept taking its place. Why is it that the more these images appeared, the further I seemed to go from her, the lonelier I got?

Each day more difficult than the one before.

Each day a new image.

Each image another extinct possibility.

What's happening? Is it that I'm only seeing now what I could not see then? What is this horrific side to seeing that in seeing her as she was before her death I failed to see the Chachcho from after her death? If only I had seen her absence while she was present before me, I would have held her tight and not let the flames consume her.

When the flashing images of a person start to surround you, you know that the person is gone. And even being with all these images of her is nothing like being with her alone. They appear and disappear, and when they appear again, someone else's image also starts glimmering within them.

It's becoming impossible now, to be with Chachcho without being with Lalna as well!

If not this Lalna, then the one whom the people of Laburnum House called Chachcho's Kashmiri apple. When once, in my childishness, I had said, 'Chachcho is a jamun.'

'And that one's her Kashmiri apple...' they'd laughed and said, and I had laughed too.

'She was so tiny when she first arrived,' Chachcho would tease. 'Now look at this fat queen.'

'Go away, I won't wear this.' Lalna was cross. 'You called me ugly.'

'I called you beautiful,' Chachcho would try to appease her.

'But your eyes are bigger. Like a long slice of mango.'

'But your ass is bigger. Like the base of a tanpura!'

They had a play-acting programme once.

Chachcho's silk saris are lying behind the tank on the roof. They've tied their petticoats up around their breasts. Now they will put aalta on their feet, henna patterns on the palms of their hands, and red bindis on their foreheads.

And I am holding the bowl of aalta, helping them wash and wipe their hands, going down and up, fetching this, returning that, happily doing the little chores.

Fragrant garlands of harsingar around their arms, waist, neck and ankles.

I too have a garland, which has become squashed in some places and become wet and orange.

Wispy, susurrating saris are being pleated quickly – one on one, one on one – then being held down and ironed.

I've been turned into a little swami baba with two chunnis.

Two more lace chunnis are taken out next. Turning their backs to me, Chachcho and Lalna take off their blouses and tie the sheer, sequined muslin chunnis with a big knot between their breasts. It's as if Shakuntala and Damayanti have descended from the calendars, swinging their plaits braided with marigold over their flimsy, shiny clothes. Taking me in their laps, they coo – 'How sweet he looks! And what about us?'

'Let's sing,' they say, and start singing as if the roof is both their stage and their audience.

Jawaani ghaate mein ganwaai koi baalam ko de do taar. I'm losing my youth for nothing, won't somebody call my lover… Their throats open, their soft notes swirling lustily through the air, they would start giving a beat to the words, almost dancing.

They'd let me sing with them. They'd let me hold their hands and sway.

❖

Looking from a distance now, I've started seeing the nephew I used to be, hovering almost invisibly between the two girls, all stubbornness and affection.

Their playfulness pulls him to them, unknowingly. Though silent, he is still a part of their whisperings.

'Why do you have to walk in the middle,' Lalna would tease.

Chachcho would lovingly stroke her nephew's head.

'There's no space in the middle,' Lalna would cling to Chachcho.

'There is,' the nephew would say, pushing her.

'But I knew your Chachcho first, before you were even born,' Lalna would thumb her nose at him.

'Ask her, did Chachcho take you in her lap when she was this small,' Chachcho would pull her nephew into her lap and help him win the argument.

'Okay, I get it, I mean nothing to you,' Lalna would get upset.

'No, no, you do,' the nephew would try to appease her.

'Is that so?' Chachcho would tickle him.

'But less than me,' the nephew would say, jumping up.

And like a little animal, he'd burrow with his head and make space for himself between the two. To have both of them equally, or to push them apart a little?

The question will not leave me. It keeps raising its head in my lonely heart: Did I want to separate them even then?

I've come up to the roof where the last rays of the sun fill up the emptiness around me, where there's space enough for old images and new questions to appear and disappear.

I'm startled. As if I've forgotten, like in the old days, that Uncle has sent me – 'Go, call them down, but don't tell them I said so.'

'What are these big secrets they can talk about only on the roof?' he'd ask his nephew.

'What are these big secrets you can talk about only on the roof?' I would ask them, without mentioning Uncle.

The two women are sitting in the smoky darkness. They sit their nephew between them and cover him with their shawl. He doesn't understand why they cry and laugh, he isn't concerned. He has fallen asleep, lulled by their voices like twinkling stars and their warm smell of milk and ghee.

Uncle is still waiting downstairs. He starts taking out stuff from his trunk and making a pile on the bed – an eyebrow pencil, a bottle of nail polish, a lipstick, a purse, a watch, a lacy nylon nighty, a frilly housecoat, a radio transistor, a plastic butterfly to wear in one's hair, flowers, leaves, a lighter – as if he only had to make this colourful mountain and his old doll would come down to join the heap. His pink polythene bundles lie ready. The stench of railway stations rises, wrapped in coal, from his clothes.

He will go to Calcutta, then to Hong Kong.

He won't come to the roof.

'On the roof, we talk... of things only girls talk about... that we can talk about only on the roof... understand?'

Murmuring, as if in a dream.

The nephew is sleeping.

Am I awake?

Am I him?

Was I really him?

I look around the roof.

In this light, it looks strangely unappealing. Peeling, perhaps, from the heat after the rains.

Some people have already painted over their portion of the roof. The trees nearby are spattered with paint. Only the next year's rains will wash them clean. What celebration are they preparing for?

Suddenly, all I can see is stains. Old stains from seepage on the walls, crow and pigeon shit on the water tanks, betel juice stains in the stairway – all of Laburnum House a leper. Entangled within the TV and telephone wires hanging out of its windows and the rusted pipes going down from its roof.

This can't be the roof of that nephew's Laburnum House.

His roof was one that had its wings spread out, as if it

were the airplane he would hop on to as soon as he grew up, to turn into an Englishman – a vilayati-babu – and fly away!

❖

Should I laugh at my dream just because it stood on a foundation that never existed? But who ever looks at foundations? Dreams are the stuff of happy illusions. All the hopes and joys of my childhood were built on my illusions.

At that time, there were only two homes in all of Laburnum House that had some connection to a foreign land, not like today when every Tom, Dick and Harry has been abroad! One was ours, where Uncle used to go regularly to Hong Kong, and my heart was waiting to fly to my country overseas! The other was Ms Boniface's, who was a pure Englishwoman from the time of the Raj, a retired Inspectress of Schools. Her skylight was broken and only I was foolhardy enough to run up to it and, surrounded by the other children, stick my dick in and let loose a stream! At which her Pomeranian would start jumping and barking at the skylight like a wind-up toy, but I'd run off with my gang of admirers to some other corner of the roof, my stature grown higher, even in my own eyes.

There I'd spread out my magic carpet of dreams and, lying down on it like a white nawab, fly here and there.

'You're filling his head with trash,' Lalna would scold. 'Behen-ji, give him a tight slap.' But Chachcho would never slap me. And with great condescension, which was childish to begin with but grew ever more sophisticated, I would, like all our neighbours crazy about foreign lands, think, what's so great about this country – laziness, cunning, disorder? What son of man would want to stay here, I'd think, my chest puffed up.

And I would become a man.

In which becoming, there always lurked the thought of women!

I remember Kamala, who'd come to a house in the far corner of the mohalla to give tuitions on Saturday, and return somewhere on Monday. Paresh and I would bend over the skylight to her room late at night and watch her dance to English music in the light of a red-shaded lamp. And in our line of vision, she'd sometimes flash her behind, sometimes her breasts, sometimes her bare arms, as if playing hide and seek. Sometimes she'd remove a piece of clothing, sometimes quickly cover up. This flashing spark of a girl!

And then there was the one who was convent-educated and fair and who'd come to meet me behind the tank.

'She wants to marry me,' I told Paresh.

'Man, you and your vilayati charms,' he kicked me, envious yet wishing me well.

But... Do I have to tell this story too? We broke up. And anyway, her man-eating ways, which I had loved initially, eventually started leaving me strangely exhausted. She found the roof hard, so she'd always want to be on top. Would I not find the roof hard too? And I would feel like an upturned cockroach, lying on my back, gripped by the legs of some powerful creature that rode me and pushed me around, half-dead. It wasn't good for my libido.

'It's okay, man,' Paresh patted my back when we broke up. 'What do you want, a wife or a whore?'

The truth was that she left me, but Paresh and I decided that I left her.

When her memories troubled me, I'd go to the roof and grab Sona as she made the beds for our next-door neighbours. Once, as I was passing by, she had spread out the mattress and sheet, set the pillows down, smoothed the creases with her hand, and with a quick glance all around, lay down on her masters' bed. Then I appeared before her. How frightened she was!

Later, whenever I went to her as she made the beds, she would smile and flirt with me. I would lend a hand and, while I helped her, we'd keep touching each other.

We became so used to it that for years, even in pitch darkness, we could recognize each other solely by touch. As if we had, with our own hands, created each other's bodies out of the darkness.

Lalna didn't need to touch anything to find out. One day, when the lights went out, she showed up. 'If I see any more of this sahib-ness, manliness, vilayati-ness, I'll fling you back into the hell where you came from.'

❖

Where I came from – that phrase attached itself to me like a little tail and kept growing longer and longer as I grew older and taller, and my attempts to keep it coiled and hidden away became the vicious joke that is my life.

The sun is harsh today, but only by going up to the roof will I be able to shake off this mortification.

I'm climbing the stairs when the door to the roof opens.

Lalna. Her face hidden somewhere behind starched white sheets that the harsh sunlight has carved into mountains and valleys.

I don't move.

The sun-scented mountain steps back and leans to one side so that I may pass.

As I advance, I'm irritated by the thought that her eyes

can watch me safely from behind that mountain. Mocking this vilayati-babu's cautious steps. Theatrically, with an exaggerated politeness, the mountain leans even further away. And even today, I'm afraid and want to check if my fly's not open.

'I'm not saying this, people are. I don't believe it, but people care,' I stammered under Chachcho's gaze. 'She's not of our status, then why…'

Chachcho kept looking at me.

'That Uncle was wrong in giving her shelter in this house,' I kept speaking, though afraid.

Chachcho and the look.

'Didn't you scold me once, saying I shouldn't have sold them even if I wasn't reading them?'

Chachcho still the same.

'The books, I mean,' I shouted loudly.

Chachcho slammed the cup down so hard that hot tea splashed all over me.

'But you never asked how your pearl necklace became shorter, did you?' I whimpered, seeing the look of concern on her face.

Sick and tired of this woman.

'You call that a woman? For shame!' people clamoured. 'See how she behaves!'

'Women should be quiet and restrained, otherwise they'll regret it. Your breasts don't hurt when you jump, do they?' Uncle laughed obscenely as he told me. 'Will you be scared of going out alone at night? Any danger to you? If there was no difference, wouldn't God have made them just like you? A woman's not a woman if she doesn't behave like one.'

'See if she doesn't make you cry.' I couldn't bring myself to tell Chachcho what people said.

That non-woman who'd make both Chachcho and her nephew cry while flying kites.

The nephew's crying loudly because Lalna refuses to give him the line. Her eyes are watering because of the bright sunlight piercing through the cloud cover. Lips pursed, she spools and unspools the line, churning the cloud-filled sky.

Chachcho – who doesn't fly kites, who doesn't jump or shout – is standing at a distance, rubbing her eyes with her fists as if she wants to crush them. They're red and filled with tears, her clenched fists are wet.

Lalna laughs. She has pinned a big, green plastic bag to her head, like an umbrella to protect herself from the sun. From where I stand today, she looks like a kite.

❖

Old visions return, as if they'd only been premonitions so far but are now, finally, taking place.

Maybe this is how it always is. Things don't really happen when they're happening. They happen later. When a storm within links them up to the larger picture.

When it's happening, we step around it in some strange bewilderment. Later, we fall right into the heart of it.

It's an itch we can feel in our skin.

Being born to the wrong mother...

Staying in and belonging to this place instead of a foreign land...

Someone's death...

All premonitions that have now become a reality.

I stop at a skylight. From within, the yellow light of a bulb. The roof, a dark grief enveloping that world.

Chachcho isn't down there. The hand on the teapoy, near

the ashtray, isn't hers. The hand thoughtfully plays with a pack of Four Squares. The thoughts turn into smoke and rise up. The one blowing these smoke rings into the air isn't Chachcho.

It's Lalna.

I press myself up against the skylight, the way I used to in my carefree childhood.

My friend Paresh would be pressed up here with me. I had shouted 'times' because I needed to use the bathroom. I went downstairs and ran back up immediately. We bent over the skylight, joined in unbreakable friendship.

'By god!' Paresh screamed.

The lower half of Chachcho's body, sitting on a chair, jerking slowly, rhythmically.

'Look at how your Uncle's sitting,' he burst out, 'spread wide open.' He opened his legs and flopped down on the roof.

I saw Lalna's back and head too. Bent in front of Chachcho's chair, moving her head swiftly, left and right, left and right, lightning falling from her open hair.

'Ai hai,' Paresh said eagerly, 'and see how Lalna's licking like it's chicken curry. Come...' he pulled me down, 'get started,' he said lasciviously.

I didn't tell him that Uncle was in Hong Kong.

I remember now that when I had gone down to the bathroom, Chachcho had been squeezing out orange juice and Lalna had been mopping the floor.

But so what, no story is untrue.

Or true.

It just keeps combining in different ways. The same things from different angles. And all around, the swirling haze of intervening years.

'Oh, your Uncle's so lucky,' Paresh would tell me. 'But what do you care? You can go to Hong Kong whenever you want, where the girls, I've heard, are so skilled they can cut bananas with their you-know-what into perfectly even slices...'

Why Hong Kong? I wanted to go to Britain, where anything and everything could be mine, not just girls and bananas.

Suddenly it's as if someone has pushed a mirror in front of me, and I find not myself but my Uncle looking back. Who has told me time and again, in great detail, his dreams of money – not foreign lands. He's quiet now. Because I've asked him what he would do when he had earned all that money.

What would he do? He looks at me blankly. What would he do? He repeats like a broken record. What would he do? As if he's asking me.

'Then,' he says flatly, 'then I can do anything.'

❖

'We're men, we can do anything!' When Paresh would say things like that, I'd be so disgusted by the ridiculous gossip flying around Laburnum House that I wouldn't tell him how, let alone Lalna, Uncle wouldn't even go to Chachcho. It was Chachcho who'd go to him.

When, at night, I'd insist on staying between Chachcho and Lalna for fear of being left out of their conversation and, eventually, fall asleep.

When Uncle would come, still smelling a little of the railway station, and carry me away to the living room and rock me back to sleep in his arms.

Half-asleep, half-conscious, I knew what would happen next. Chachcho would come after me.

Or after him?

I'd wake up but pretend to sleep.

She'd open the door gently and I'd feel the warmth of the lamp that stayed lit all night on my closed eyelids.

I would try to stop breathing, thinking that, in the dark of night, air would rush out of my lungs loudly, like a battle cry.

I would think that it was now Chachcho who drank, while Uncle had stopped drinking.

Uncle would pretend to be fast asleep.

Chachcho would come closer and closer, my stifled breath would tell me.

Her breath is hot. She's touching Uncle. Angrily. Pulling him. Climbing on top of him. Scratching him. And Uncle – as if he'd been sleeping and was woken up – is annoyed, disgusted. He refuses her, shakes off her hand, pushes her off himself. The bed shakes, she falls away and pounces back like a wounded animal, both of them hissing violently.

'Why not?' says Chachcho's hurt voice.

'Because I want a woman, not you,' Uncle answers.

Did I hear these things just once? Time after time, I remember seeing with half-open eyes – Chachcho, hurt, flung away like a snake, panting, fuming.

And then…

My eyes are closed, but I know where Uncle's hand is and what it's doing, to spite Chachcho who looks on, sad, seething, abandoned. If Chachcho sobs, the hand will move even faster, and the whole bed will shudder at this grotesque triumph of man over woman.

❖

I feel something free itself from me and begin prancing around on the roof. As if some possibility that couldn't come alive then has come alive now.

A part of me is happy that Chachcho and Uncle didn't do all that I, an ignorant child, had heard people say Uncle did with both women. So there was no stain on Chachcho. Nothing icky. The ascetic Chachcho, who hid away more and more of her body every day under that plain-bordered sari.

'Poor Chachcho,' people would say. 'You'd never hear a peep out of her about her husband's ways, and now she's even taking care of that other woman out of pity for her swollen stomach.' Chachcho would be respectfully invited to every occasion, happy or sad or festive. And when Lalna arrived with her, she too was humbly accepted – for Chachcho's sake.

A true woman is one who understands the heart of her man. Forgives him. Lets him return after he has strayed.

And Uncle had come back home after closing down his business, but could that be called a return? The reason for his failing health, it turned out, was late-stage diabetes. And Chachcho, clearly laughing, had said, 'What a way to become sweeter!'

Uncle heard her, but didn't reply.

'Quiet,' Lalna would tell Chachcho when she'd see him approaching, and Chachcho would turn her face away from him, and he'd turn his face away from Lalna.

I turn my face away from these memories and shake my head hard to empty my mind of them.

Someone has passed away. Someone so dear. I should be grieving. Sombre and silent, inside and out. Praying.

Instead, there's commotion – inside and outside.

Children playing with a ball. The creaking of bicycle wheels. Scooters. Cars. Horns. The flutter of birds' wings. It shouldn't be like this.

How do I forget it all and stand with my head lowered in a corner, quietly, feeling nothing?

Knowing only this – that you no longer live. Why should I toss your past on the rooftop, like a ball of wool, ravelling and unravelling?

I try to sit silently, but then this commotion makes its way into my heart through unknown passages and the ball of wool slips out from my hands. It rolls and spins on the roof in shapes that are uncomprehended, unknown, unspoken, unseen, unlived… Real? Are they real?

Those shapes are not the shapes of my jamun-stained sorrow, but the waving, flapping outlines of something else.

I try to sit silently, silent in every fibre of my being. Reminding every fibre of what it is, perhaps, forgetting – that Chachcho is gone, Chachcho has died. Like a mantra for meditation. Om.

Om.

Ommmmm.

But what trickery is this? Om was Uncle's name!

❖

Uncle's trips to Hong Kong had almost stopped. Or maybe he thought Hong Kong was in the toilet, because whenever you saw him that's where he'd be heading!

'Sugar's just an excuse!' Chachcho would smile scornfully. Uncle would hear her, but she wasn't speaking to him.

She had always been quiet, but whether people knew it or not, I knew that this wasn't her usual quietness. Chachcho had decided to not talk to Uncle.

It was nothing to be ashamed of. Every home in Laburnum House had a host of people not talking to each other. Members of the same family would stop talking for a day or two or more – it was an everyday thing. And sometimes the reason would be forgotten but the not-talking would go on for life! Or to start talking to one person, you'd have to stop talking to another. But there was nothing in this not-talking that would break families apart. They'd stay together, they'd stay the same.

Paresh was a typical example. He was good at math and wanted to study it at a big university. His father wanted him to study history and try for the IAS – one couldn't make a good living by studying math. Such a small thing, and they stopped talking over it.

So, ever since he finished high school, Paresh and his father haven't talked. 'Why hasn't he come downstairs, call him,' his father would say and his mother would call him, 'Paresh!' All three would sit and eat at the same table. His mother would talk to her son and to her husband. His father would talk to his wife. He would talk to his mother. The food would be great.

Sometimes I'd go to his house. His father would tease me, 'So babu-vilayati, when are you sending us tickets from London?' Paresh would laugh, 'So babu-vilayati, hasn't Queen Elizabeth herself arranged to welcome you?' And all the while they'd keep their mutual silence intact.

When Paresh went out of town to get admitted to a big university, his father went with him, and they stayed together in a hotel. While he sat for the scholarship exam, his father waited in the hall outside, pacing up and down. When, on the train back, he went to the toilet, his father picked up and examined the question paper. But talk? No way!

Paresh's father chose his wife for him – but even when he got married and she came to live with them, the situation didn't change.

A father and son here, sisters-in-law there. A brother and sister here, a husband and wife there. Not-talking was everywhere. This is how joint families stayed joint. This is how unbreakable the non-speaking relationships were.

In our house, it was Chachcho and Uncle.

'Give me something sweet,' Uncle would come to me after dinner.

'You aren't allowed,' I'd say softly, an eye on Chachcho in the next room.

'Look, if I don't eat sweets, I get indigestion,' he'd whisper, following my gaze.

'She's forbidden it.'

'Then give me a bit of jaggery.'

'It's locked in the cupboard.'

'Some sugar then.'

Seeing me straighten up, he'd understand that Chachcho was coming towards us.

'Why are you standing here?' she'd ask me sternly.

Uncle would look at the ants on the floor and mumble something incomprehensible, and I'd come up with an excuse – 'He's looking for dysentery pills,' for example.

'Is he gone?' Chachcho would turn away and ask.

Uncle would go back to his room and sit beside his trunk which contained countless bank papers and share certificates. Chachcho had even made him add Lalna's name to some of them. And that's why, we found out one day, that so much of it had already been encashed.

❖

My anger knows no bounds. Why do we find out about such things only later? Why not when they're actually happening? The way we only notice a centipede after it's engorged and drunk on our blood, not while it has been merrily sucking away!

Or is it the future that's cheating us? We let it fill up our insides and close our eyes to look inwards, waiting, while staying blind to the present that's out there.

But I know who'll be out there when I open my eyes.

She has seen me.

And when she sees me, even if my eyes are closed, she passes by strangely, as if she can't decide whether to turn towards me or to go straight past. As if she can't decide what's more respectful: looking straight ahead, or lowering her head a little while raising her eyes towards me.

So her shoulders sometimes jump towards me as if wanting to separate from her body, while her head goes straight ahead. Sometimes her head wants to come here while the rest of her body turns away. A strange limping gait, undecided and crooked.

I cautiously open my eyes, turning away from the future inside me, which is now my past. Lalna goes past with henna thickly smeared upon her hair like a green towel, forcing its fragrance into my grief.

I close my eyes as if that can stop her odious smell from invading my senses.

The voices of children coming back from school reach me, echoing sunnily, and images of school bags and uniforms swim into my vision.

I can hear her gossiping with the maid.

'So you've seen Delhi too?' the maid asks, as if it were the moon, not Delhi.

'It has two forts,' Lalna says. 'The Red Fort and the Old Fort.'

She explains the difference – 'One has a flea market, the other has a zoo!'

I sneak away without letting her see me. To the roof. Her stubborn voice follows me for a long time, though.

Why does the sound of her voice fill me with some unknown fear and make me stop short? As if there's something more lying in wait behind this inane chatter – something serious, something nagging, that's weak for now but will gain strength and soon I'll be completely in its grip.

Gravel has been poured over the melting tar on the roof, so that it doesn't stick to people's slippers.

She has found me. I know, even without turning, that she's been following me.

From the corners of my eyes, I see her spreading freshly washed wheat out to dry. I want to touch it, feel its dampness on my hands. I want the grains to stick to my palms once more, for the first time since my childhood.

I've started recognizing the touch of that unknown fear. As if it's trying to warn me: You're returning to the wrong embrace!

I won't turn. I'm just standing there, when a group of langurs loudly descends from the jamun tree to the roof, spreading purple jamun stains with their feet.

Langurs, more langurs. Of all sizes and all ages. Male and female, young and old, new-borns even. Some sitting quietly, some somersaulting. The expression on their faces is not one of victory or defeat, but of saintly detachment. I feel like telling someone, but no one's here.

The jamun branches are surrounded by a makeshift brick wall. Maybe the people in the house below are trying to claim the tree, its branches and its fruit as their own, because they've already laid claim to its trunk and roots outside their window.

When I was a child, the roof belonged to everyone, and the trees belonged to the roof.

But nothing can stop the langurs. They're even eating up the new leaves on the jamun tree.

On that makeshift brick wall, a female langur sits holding a baby in her lap. The same Buddhist face, the same detached eyes.

My interest is piqued. How joyfully the other monkeys launch themselves off her head and jump from this side and that. As if she's part of the wall.

I hear a muffled scream behind me. Lalna.

All of a sudden I realize that the baby is dead.

Does its mother not know? She sits with the child, impassively. When the baby's head shakes from the impact of the other monkeys leaping, she steadies it without looking.

She sits, and will keep on sitting, as if death is just a sleep from which her child will awake any moment now.

I read somewhere that religion was born from sin, and philosophy from grief.

She'll keep sitting there with her child in her lap till there's not one bit of warmth left in its body. And only when it's absolutely cold will her attachment, her hope, die.

❖

When I came downstairs, I felt as if I'd left the roof far, far behind. There was only the dim echo of its distant sounds, bearing messages of separation and longing.

I stood in the verandah, raising my head sometimes at

those sounds coming from afar, then lowering it again as if meditating to empty myself.

All around me are the same old rooms, but the sight of the freshly washed curtains troubles me, as if the touch of this new hand will push away every familiar, comfortable feeling.

There's always a sewing machine in the verandah these days. Lalna has oiled its rusted parts and has started using it again. Now I have to see her here as well – moistening the thread with spit, then trying to thread the machine's needle for hours on end. Doing it over and over as if the thread was a needle and the needle's eye the eye of someone she wanted to blind.

I was worried that I'd unwittingly end up offering to help her.

She's always had a way of making people do what she wants without saying a word.

I wonder why the rainy days from my childhood come to mind – the rains are long gone…

The Lalna of old times speaks up: 'What a downpour!'

She was telling Chachcho. 'Isn't it, Behen-ji?'

It wasn't just small talk – she had a plan!

'Just the weather for pakoras, isn't it, Behen-ji?'

Chachcho was sitting at this very machine, sewing. Even now I can hear the sounds. Her hand moving round and round and the cloth leaping and dancing under her hand, a little to the left, a little to the right, before slipping to the floor.

'Should I make some, Behen-ji?' Her tone guileless.

'Give me a minute, then I'll have to change the thread anyway,' Chachcho explained apologetically.

'No, no, you finish. I don't make them too bad either.

Tell me what kind you'd like. Green chilli? Onion, potato, or eggplant?' Chewing her nails and gathering spit in her mouth as if she'd use it to make the pakoras!

'Where's the gram flour kept? The same place as the other flours?' This nail needing more chewing.

Chachcho got up, Lalna pretended not to see. Chachcho sieved the flour in the kitchen, Lalna was busy with her nails. The smell of hot oil in the air, but Lalna's nose couldn't tell. And then Chachcho came out with tea and pakoras, just as Lalna finished her work and started rising from her chair.

'What's this? I was just about to go make them.' She sits down again.

But why's there a smile on my lips?

That same smell – pakoras! My stomach rumbles in hunger – or greed. My feet start moving of their own accord towards the bed beside the sewing machine. I lean on the bed and am starting to recline, when an anger flares up inside me once more – is this what I've sunk to?

My hands automatically pick up the cup of tea that has appeared on a tray near me. Why does the steam rising from it smell of pakoras?

A plate approaches from behind me and stops at the tray. Ah, pakoras made from the leaves of arvi! I'd forgotten how much I loved them.

Tears fill my eyes as my mouth waters. Am I forgetting you, Chachcho?

❖

This is how it happens: your memories of someone get besieged by so many things that, eventually, they have to give in.

Am I losing Chachcho to this array of delicious food that somehow keeps finding me?

Where did this jackfruit come from, out of season? And just for me. I stare at it as if it's going to eat me up.

I rip up the chapatti angrily and refuse to eat it. I keep staring at the man-eating jackfruit.

Still greedy.

Still angry.

Or is something else happening here? Is something that happened long ago finally starting to become real?

Am I being given birth to once more?

Frightened, I start eating. And being frightened only makes the jackfruit taste better!

My real birth. I want to laugh and laugh. But the laughter that's jumping around the pieces of jackfruit is Uncle's.

A laugh laughed long ago – when I was tearing open a pack of foreign chocolates with the confidence of being vilayati, unlike the Indians around me – but only now becoming real. Finding its target as it dances around the dining table saying, 'Vilayati? Really? You and vilayati? You're not even related to those you think are kin!'

If it's time for that laughter now, I fear it may also be time for my birth. A time I hoped would never come. But it has come. And if I am born, will all that shame, all that disgrace, all that gossip on the roof, all that history-less history attach itself to me too?

Helpless, I keep eating.

Does everything that's ever happened lie in wait till it can become real and grab you by the throat? Why does life not just go past, leaving us untouched? Let the blinds remain drawn over my consciousness, let me sleep.

Surrounded by all this delicious food, I'm becoming

weaker and weaker. It's stirring up a greed within me, but also an abject kind of affection.

I want to stop eating the food she makes but, if I stop, her stubborn, tray-pushing hand will open my mouth and go down my throat! I know that it will try everything to have its way.

Hate. I want hatred for her to fill my heart. As if I'm afraid that some other emotion buried under all my hatred for her – something softer, with a touch of pity, or the memories of childhood closeness – might start thinking it's time to resurface.

Save me, Chachcho, from all that's happened in this life and is threatening to become real.

Who knows what will be revealed when these old sandstorms settle.

Think of something else, I tell my anxious heart, think of laughter, of crying, anything else. I get up defiantly, leaving the food half-eaten. Don't be silly now, choose your mother once and for all, the one who gave shelter to your soul, not the one who is a hurt, blemished, diseased part of your body, whom you're not talking to and should never talk to.

This is what needs to happen, this is the only way life can go on. My decision to not talk to her needs to be irreversible, the way Uncle's coma was irreversible, the way Chachcho's death was irreversible, the way Lalna's return to this house after being thrown out...

The thought rattles me so badly that I wish I couldn't think at all, and in that little moment of fright, I pick up the newspaper and read aloud –

'The next big earthquake will hit Northern India'

– forgetting that she'll have silently come and sat behind me, ready to get me what I need before I knew I needed it.

I haven't spoken to her, but she'll pretend that I have, and will quickly turn it into the start of a conversation –

'When?'

II

'When?' slipped out of my mouth automatically.

If it hadn't been such a small word I would have stopped it!

Quickly, I composed myself, hoping that the lids he had placed on his ears would stop the 'when'!

But he continued speaking, to get over the awkwardness perhaps. 'It says here that it could come any time in the next hundred years.'

And to smooth over my slip-up, I had to continue speaking in a natural tone too, 'So there's still a hundred years, no?'

He got irritated. 'If it comes tomorrow, that's also some time in the next hundred years.'

We could have laughed. But since we didn't laugh, we had to get irritated. Even I did. I got up slowly, lifting the chair with me – no, no, no, don't make a sound – and stood like that, bent forward, intending to quietly move it aside. And for a moment it felt as if it wasn't a chair but the filthy commode at the cinema where Behen-ji and I would crouch and pee without sitting.

If not for me and the burqa I brought, how would your Chachcho ever have stepped out of Laburnum House and known the bliss of peeing in a dirty stinking latrine?

I'd had it up to here with her regular routine of questions. 'Then? Then what happened? When did he find out that he wasn't the dacoit's son?' With having to tell her the whole story, scene by scene. With having to sing her the songs. Describing the heroine's tight kameez, getting it made from the tailor. And then wearing it, for her pleasure.

But where was the pleasure in that, Bitwa? Your Chachcho's eyes would blaze. She'd be so jealous that she'd pinch my arms until they were swollen, saying, 'What's it to you? You're invisible, you can go anywhere. If I go, everyone will notice.'

Not invisible – ignored. When neither Behen-ji nor Om Babu said a thing, who in Laburnum House would have the courage to speak? And if they did speak, it wouldn't be just Lalna they were maligning but these two respectable people as well! How could they eat this 'Kashmiri apple' ripening in their midst? And if they couldn't eat it, what was the point of drooling over it? So silence was better, blindness was wise.

And even if their gaze did stray in my direction, it was as if I wasn't there.

Oh, how I loved that gaze! Insects are afraid of being seen because they'll be squashed. I, on the other hand, would step out like a lioness. Let them worry about my claws! I will dance. I will sing. If I feel like it, I will scratch my thighs. Why shouldn't I, if they itch? Should I kill myself to get their respect? When they can't even see me, how will they see me scratching myself?

'Come, let's you make you invisible,' I had an idea. I went and got her a burqa. 'Now you can come out with me. I'm invisible, and any friend of mine is invisible too.'

My friend nodded happily.

She'd dress up in a skin-tight kameez, with six-inch danglers in her ears and her feet in shiny high heels. Then she'd throw a burqa on top.

Even now, the people of Laburnum House lock their doors only between night and early morning, while they sleep. Coming and going from one house to another, from one roof to another, is possible all day.

Perhaps even now people meet secretly. Perhaps there are still women who go to the roof, after their children have gone to school and their husbands to work, and descend into someone else's empty house to exit by the backdoor and catch a rickshaw. For no reason. Secretly. Not from the big main gate of Laburnum House, but jumping over or pressing through the shrubbery out back.

Jumping! An act bursting with joy. When you jump, your heart and body thrum and thrill. Walls are jumped over. Hedges, roofs, thresholds, borders, the moon... And immediately a joyous laughter bursts out from under the burqa, a laughter that cannot be suppressed even though you're afraid someone might hear.

That's a laugh you can never laugh, Bitwa. To laugh like that you'll need to be a girl. A girl who is always naked. So naked that she has to wear heaps of clothes, layer on layer – and then cover it all up with a burqa. Only when that naked girl laughs can you hear that beautiful sound.

How can you understand the laughter of that naked girl, Bitwa?

I have moved away from him. But he probably thinks I'm still there, undeterred, never planning to get up!

My eyes focus on his back as slowly, step by step, I move backwards, invisibly, soundlessly. I reach the door to the room that he thinks was only his Chachcho's room.

I feel like pulling a face behind his back, like sticking my tongue out! What do you know of our friendship? Oh Bitwa, my little jealous child, your Chachcho and I were childhood friends. Childhood friends who had seen each other's dreams, and that's why we hated each other – but so what?

I open his Chachcho's kohl box and pick up the silver applicator. My heart begins to laugh.

❖

He's stopped talking to me again. As if conversation ceases when you shut your mouth. But I've decided that I'll have conversations with him day and night – so what if they're all in my head? And I'll make him say all that he's been trying so hard not to say. Even if it's just in my head.

Behen-ji's not around any more. It's just you and me. And if we don't talk to each other, we might as well just die.

Whenever I see him, I take a break from work and follow him like a cat so that he doesn't find out. Because if he finds out, he'll puff his face up like a pumpkin and any desire I have to talk to him will fizzle out. Then how will he say what I want him to say?

I look for him, slowly, stealthily.

He's sitting in the verandah, swatting at mosquitos, his neck sunken like a sleeping crane's. But just then he raises his head and looks around warily before letting it sink back again, reassured.

I go and sit in our room – Behen-ji's and mine – so that I can keep an eye on two places at once, on him and on that window through which Behen-ji now looks in, not out.

In my head, I grab hold of Bitwa and turn him to face me, then make him speak. Pure imagination!

'Lalna…'

He always called me by my name.

'Yes, Bitwa.'

'Lalna…'

'Right, Bitwa…'

'Lalna…'

'Say it once more, Bitwa…'

'Lalna…'

I take a deep breath, turn towards the window and sigh. He spoke my name!

He lights a cigarette. Its smoke looks like the surface of a water body from which the gathered mosquitos start rising, going far away from his puffed-up pumpkin face.

But my sigh of relief turns into a cry of regret. Why can't he turn around and give me a drag as well!

He flicks ash from his cigarette onto the floor as if the verandah is an ashtray. Does he think he's free to be dirty now that Behen-ji's no more? Otherwise he would have hollered – Ashtray!

Why? Who's this person named Ashtray? Me or your Chachcho, you prince!

At this, he sighs. 'Prince? Of what kingdom?' That's what you want to say, right?

Why? Did we spare any effort in treating you like one?

'Lalna…' His pained voice from the verandah.

'Yes, Bitwa.' I've also become sad.

'You lied.'

'Yes, Bitwa.'

'Why did you lie?'

'Because you wanted that lie.'

'You ruined my future.' In the dark verandah, his shoulders shake and, for the billionth time, my hands move guiltily to comfort him, as if I'd really done something.

But I correct myself in the nick of time. I make a face – 'Babu-vilayati!'

He's sinking into the darkness.

'Why?' I burst out angrily. All the anger I've been holding back. 'You're not from Hong Kong – am I responsible for that? And even if you were, you wouldn't automatically become an Englishman – am I responsible for that too?'

'But,' I put him in the witness box and fix him with a stare, 'did you really want to be vilayati, or did you just want to run away from all the things that no one said but everyone knew?'

'Why curse me?' My shoulders shake too. 'Did I ever tell you? Did I ever claim any right over you? Go, you have my blessings, now go – to anyone, anywhere, I don't care.'

But all he wants to do is cry. It's no fun talking to him today.

❖

Hurried and strained, he stamps up and down the stairs. Up to the roof, down to the house. Down to the house, up to the roof. To get away from me and be close to Behen-ji? To get away from me so that he can't be close to me? Or to just be close to Behen-ji?

I follow him. Carefully, in a way that lets me hide when I want to and show myself if I want to!

Not to claim any right over Bitwa. But over this house, over this roof. You twerp, you weren't even born when we used to come here – Behen-ji and I. So does that make this roof ours or yours? Your nose may be exactly like mine, but it was Behen-ji and me who wore clothes that measured exactly the same.

She'd bring two sets of clothes and come to the roof, as per the programme, her anklets softly tinkling.

A frightened, cautious, cat-like walk.

I'd come from that other house, now that no one would summon me for any chores.

What an exciting illusion: is someone watching? What an exciting fear: is someone listening?

But when 'Lallan ki' and Chachcho have gone to sleep downstairs, what'll happen? Lalna and Ambika Behen-ji will meet upstairs, fresh as daisies. They will take their slippers off at the door. They will move a bare foot towards the roof, then place it down. Cool to touch, the roof will fill their soles.

That's the first time when the laugh you can never laugh will burst forth. Are the ghosts of those two girls up there? Who come alive at every taste, every touch, every smell?

'What did you bring?'

'Sugarcane.'

Hidden behind the laburnum branches, two apparitions would change. Turning clothes that had been acquired at weddings and packed away to rot in boxes into the pretty costumes of a stage play.

How beautiful we were.

And how beautiful was the roof. Scattering countless shadows for us to disappear into. We'd skin the sugarcane with our teeth, fill our mouths with its sweet juice, and talk and talk.

'I never told anyone…'

'Who would you tell?'

'Don't tell anyone.'

'Who will I tell?'

'How much it must have hurt.'

'It still hurts terribly.'

We'd keep sucking at and spitting out the sugarcane, and bit by bit our friendship deepened on the roof.

On the roof, the voices of Laburnum House would come as if from afar, the way the voices from a village carry through the fog and over fields of sugarcane in winter, turning into a sweet melody when they fell in our ears.

Then why wouldn't the spirits of those two girls come to meet on the roof? To meet on the roof, or to meet the roof?

Let people say that they saw her on the roof, wearing a lehenga, crossing from here to there, leading someone or the other's son astray. When even you, Bitwa, hear only that, what can I say? I'll also start believing the same – that one's lehenga will appear to flutter, while the other's will appear to be a pair of trousers. What a boring story it would be otherwise!

Bitwa only thinks about himself. Crying and crying over the same old things – oh my past, oh my future, and oh this unwanted thing that's stuck to me...

What can I say, Bitwa? I ask for no right over the past or the future. Let me be free. Here, Behen-ji, take my rights. Here, Bitwa, take my rights. I have no rights at all – that thought used to frighten me... once upon a time...

❖

Early in the morning today, I caught a glimpse of Mr Pumpkin-face. As if it's my fault that he woke up at six-thirty! I was heading to the door, like I do every morning, after hearing the paperboy ring his bicycle-bell. At the same moment, Bitwa too decided to come get the paper, and bumped into me. So his face turned into a pumpkin!

His vilayati veneer vanished, and what was left was a proper Indian bumpkin pumpkin!

When I picked up the paper and gave it to him, he gave

me a look as if sending swarms of fiery bees my way. Buzz-buzz!

I felt like throwing the paper back on the ground. Go pick it up yourself, don't let anyone else's touch sully your morning.

Do you see, Behen-ji? I'm standing at that window again, where Behen-ji perhaps comes to peep in. Do you see, are you happy? He's still all yours, don't worry.

From the adjoining house, the smell of masala being ground wafts over, tickling my nose.

Look! How that creeper has flowered overnight. Believe it or not, it was all leaves yesterday, maybe a couple of flowers hidden here or there. But look at it now.

This is a house in mourning!

This is what a house in mourning looks like. Faces like pumpkins and flowers in full bloom, side by side.

Do you see, Behen-ji?

She sees. She wipes away my tears.

This is what a house in mourning looks like. The dead live on, the living keep dying! She comes back from another world to wipe my tears, the ones in this world remain blind.

The flowers caress the vine, the wasp caresses the wall, look Behen-ji! The wasp, and its shadow too. Such a dark and lively shadow, that if you wanted to catch the wasp you'd not know which one was real and which one unreal.

This is what a house in mourning looks like. The dead become real, the living become unreal.

Seeing the tea-tray, Bitwa has gone to sit in the verandah with a newspaper covering his face. Poor thing, he'll stay cowering behind it until he realizes that I've kept the tray and left!

The smell of halva must be tickling his nose – his nose,

which is like mine. Getting impatient, are you now? Do you want to tell me to go away before the halva grows cold?

But he can't say it. The thought makes me happy. Or is it the flowers? Maybe I should keep standing here, challenging him to say it! There's such strength in my arms that I've pinned him down – without touching him, without even being seen – immobile, inert, like a dead thing nailed to a wall!

Should I stay or should I go? Should I revel in my strength some more?

Oh, let him go to hell. I keep the tea and halva and walk away, shuffling my feet noisily. There. I've gone!

It's still warm, but look, the days are becoming shorter. I shut the screen doors and windows – these green insects, how they bite! They'll stay till Diwali.

I should sneak into his room to shut them there too. He's eating halva in the verandah right now. Me, he curses – but my food, he wolfs down!

How do I tell him not to turn the lights on at night? How do I tell him that these insects, worse than mosquitos, will rush in and not let him sleep? Such a pain, they even come in through the little cracks in the doors and windows.

Let me plug the cracks in the windows with some paper.

Ah, I can see the yellow flowers from here too!

Look at them, Bitwa, your heart will become whole again – I send a prayer from afar.

And immediately I take it back. Why bless someone when they don't want it?

Especially someone whose eyes, if they so much as get a glimpse of me by mistake, go blank – as if he were blind.

❖

How many this Lalna has blinded! Again and again, they've looked at me and refused to see me. It doesn't scare me or hurt me any more, it just makes me laugh.

But oh those first nights in this house, when I slept alone in the room by the courtyard – my heart would shudder every time the window shook and I would wonder who was throwing stones. Was it that bastard nephew out to take revenge for the slap? Or members of his gang? Or one or more of the many worthy people of the mohalla?

Yes, once upon a time, even Lalna could be frightened!

I'd lie awake, silently, as if I had nothing more to do with sleep in this life. Stay awake. Was that the sound of a stone? It's hot, but do I dare open the window? Let me turn the lights on!

Okay, now they're on. But what's this? It has become even darker outside! And someone is watching me, through a hole, through a crack, furtively.

No, no, turn the lights off. But now the darkness is a demon crouching over me!

What darkness, what demon? Your Uncle. Standing outside the door. The bolt is in place, but who knows... If the panels could be parted enough to peep through, perhaps they would part enough to let a hand snake in? Perhaps enough to unlock the door?

I jumped up and sat in the darkness, pulling the sheet over me – and the bed squeaked!

'What is it?' Om Babu asked, feigning innocence.

In all these years he'd never spoken to me!

'Why didn't you tell me?' Behen-ji scolded me. How was she to know that Lalna, who was as fearless as a tornado on the rooftop, turned into a mouse in the room by the courtyard?

After that, we started sleeping together.

Behen-ji would get up from the bed. She'd get a torch. She'd creep up close to me with hair covering her face and the lit torch in her mouth. Then she'd wake me.

The light from the torch would burst forth, red through her jamun-coloured cheeks.

I would laugh, I would be frightened. I would drag her in front of the mirror. In the torchlight, she would be on fire. I would push out my teeth from under my lips and become an ogress.

Laughter. Fright. Our images in the mirror. Rocking in pleasure.

And somewhere, a sound.

'Behen-ji, did you hear?' My teeth back in my mouth.

Squeak, squeak.

'Yes.' She'd wrap her arm around my waist.

'What is it, Behen-ji?'

'Someone's new Bata shoes. Now go to sleep.'

Bang.

'And this?'

'A door in some other house.'

Creak.

'Now?'

'Don't other houses have windows?'

Riiinnngg!

'The doorbell at this hour, Behen-ji?' I'd cower, still a bit scared.

'What? Who dares ring the doorbell when the two of us are here!'

Our whispers and murmurs and giggles would begin!

'Quiet! He'll wake up.'

'Come, let's wake him up ourselves!'

'I'll scream, and you can hold the torch in your mouth to scare him!'

In my sleep, I'd reach for Behen-ji and she would let me rest my head on her shoulder and tuck the sheets properly around me. She, the certitude in my new life – I, the freedom in hers.

Both unacceptable to Om Babu, because he didn't figure in either.

❖

'Did you speak up when I figured nowhere in his life?' Behen-ji was angry now. 'Why all this pity only when he's looking left out?'

Om Babu had started looking bereft. As if he knew that there was no place for him here, but had now begun to want a place here and nowhere else!

You weren't around then, Bitwa, just us two girls and a man who'd pretend to not see us, as if wondering how to deal with this new, unknown problem. Now when he went to Hong Kong, it was as if he was afraid of what might happen behind his back.

And if you'd been around then, Bitwa, you still wouldn't have known. These things have nothing to do with the things you learn at college or the things I learnt in my few years at school. What can devotees of tradition know about the shared tradition that two girls inherit? Then it doesn't matter if one is from a distinguished family and the other from nowhere. It doesn't matter if one lives in one place and the other in another. They have the same gushing hearts, the same bleeding bodies, the same desire to capture the colours of the rainbow.

It was the day of Holi! And Behen-ji was adamant that
since they met everyone every year, they must this year too.

Premanand-ji with his family. Shocked faces. Eyes that
didn't see me. Me, standing behind the curtain, almost a part
of it, absolutely still so that the curtain didn't so much as
quiver, afraid that otherwise the respect everyone had for
Behen-ji would be tainted.

The sort of day when Lalna herself was trying to make
Lalna invisible!

The sort of day when I was inside while everyone was
outside. Outside, celebrating. A celebration that receded
further and further away as I buried myself deeper and
deeper inside.

Behen-ji was forcing a plateful of sweet gujias into my
hands. But in trying to be invisible, I couldn't even hear
myself breathe any more.

'Enough, Lalna, enough,' Behen-ji repeated, when my
breath started thundering!

'Come now, let me clean you up,' she said.

Seating me on a stool, she started smearing my hair with
shikakai and amla. And she kept on talking. Talking to me,
bathing me, and I kept on crying. Pouring some water, she
rubbed besan into my skin. It turned into blue-red-black
grime and started flowing. She smeared some on her eyes and
nose, too, which made her start sniffling. Her conversation
was a way back into our childhood, and nothing else. Her
bathing me was a way of washing away my history, and
nothing else.

When everyone in Laburnum House came out dressed in
new clothes, I came out too, dressed up and decked up so
that for some moments a flutter ran through their eyes, and
then all of them turned blind once more.

Their eyes stopped seeing me before my very eyes!

Just the way you don't see me, Bitwa.

Just the way your Uncle didn't.

'He doesn't see me either!' Behen-ji would grumble.

She'd been very young when Om Babu married her and brought her home. One day, as he was brushing his teeth, she noticed the unevenly squished tube of toothpaste and said, 'Where I come from, I learnt to start pressing from the bottom and go neatly upwards.' Om Babu's mouth was full of foam. He didn't say anything. Eyes blazing, he picked up the tube and twisted and pressed it this way and that, spreading the paste everywhere. Then he spat out the foam and said, 'Where I come from, I learnt this.'

Om Babu thought that clarified everything – she'd been shown her place. He threw himself into making money and more money. He seemed to think that buying his wife things and more things was enough. He'd buy all sorts of rubbish and heap it upon her.

'Is this really giving?' Behen-ji would ask me. 'What has he given me?' She'd grab my hand. 'Even Bitwa I got from you.'

❖

I spring up happily as if Behen-ji has come and said, come let's go to our roof.

Did Bitwa's newspaper fall out of his hands? Did he spill his tea on seeing me run up the stairs like this?

And he's come running too. After me.

How the tables have turned!

I pretend to not have seen him. I walk happily among the swaying shadows of trees and vines. So many leaves are sprouting all around as if thousands of happy little hands are opening to give out life.

If they didn't have roots, the trees would have run too!

My slipper catches somewhere and I stumble a little. But Bitwa stumbles too! Are you the one wearing these slippers? Or has the fear that made you run up not left you yet?

Still, I'm flustered. He must think I did it on purpose, to scare him. Such cheap tricks are not my style, I'd turn and tell him if I could.

'You're getting fat,' Behen-ji would have said. But how can she say it now?

Do I find myself under the branches of the jamun tree because I thought of her?

The jamuns on the tree would get fat and ripe in the rains. Jamun-cheeked Behen-ji, in love with her new self, would come here to pick jamuns!

Did you people see her?

Don't think of anyone as just her body. Did you see the invisible spirit that walked ahead of that calm, collected body? Her feet skipping in front of Behen-ji's careful steps on the roof. The body would walk slowly, behind. In front of it that invisible spirit would run. And when Behen-ji held my hand and ran in the dark, she – the one in front of her – ran even faster! Always in front of her. Full of desires, always wanting more, tearing through her own skin to burst free!

Even when she was quietly picking jamuns, she was there, ahead of her outstretched arm – that unpermitted, unrestrained, invisible one inside her!

When the rains have gone, how can there be jamuns?

When Behen-ji has gone, what's the use of jamuns?

But there he stands, taking stock of the situation, wondering what has come over this fat woman. I search among the leaves and branches – if I see some jamuns I can pretend I came to pick them.

Dust showers upon me and a gummy liquid oozes out of the broken leaves, sticking obstinately to my fingers.

If you boil jamun leaves in water and drink it, it cures diseases of the blood. And it cures cough.

That's it! I came to get the leaves. Good! Now go, I address Bitwa silently.

Where do I keep the leaves? In the pallu? Of Behen-ji's sari!

As if I haven't already placed everything I had in it – Bitwa – my heart laughs. If I kept crying over past and future rights like all of you, then how would I walk my carefree walk? I would've kept saying, like Behen-ji, 'Not me Lalna, everyone's watching!'

So I stood myself up like a scarecrow for everyone to see, so that they couldn't badmouth Behen-ji. Ridicule? Not everyone's lucky enough to be ridiculed. The colour of ridicule is black. And the one who is ridiculed can then disappear into darkness and be free!

That roof is six steps lower than this one. Straight steps with crooked shadows. I take a few deep breaths. Cupping my hands, I climb down, when my slipper catches again and I stumble again.

Bitwa hasn't made a sound, but suddenly he is in front of me. As if to save me.

In the harsh sunlight, we stand facing each other, awkwardly. How long has it been since our eyes met like this? Unblinking. My, my, dumbstruck, are you?

Should I say it's getting hotter?

But it's getting cooler.

Should I say it's getting cooler?

Why don't you say something, Bitwa?

I wonder what he could say on this auspicious occasion and form the words for him – What a zigzag, crooked gait you have! Why don't you walk straight?

If he spoke, his voice would come out as if slipping on spit!

Zigzag. I see the shadow of the steps below. Bitwa has unknowingly suggested the perfect word. Straight steps with zigzag shadows.

Congratulations, I tell myself.

He takes out a handkerchief from his pocket. I put the jamun leaves in it, avoiding his touch.

Don't give your hanky to anyone or you'll never speak to them again – you kids had this superstition.

And that's what happened, isn't it? Who says superstitions are baseless?

So did everyone in the world give Om Babu a hanky? Is that why he stopped speaking to everyone?

The way he's looking at the steps, it seems he also remembers that this was the same place from which the handkerchief and sandal disappeared – only to be found in Om Babu's trunk after he slipped into a coma.

If he were alive, I'd say, you will live long Om Babu – both your nephew and Lalna are thinking of you at the same time!

Bitwa's shoulder is stooped in a way that suggests he wouldn't brush me off if I were to take his support to climb down. But I've started wondering whether your Uncle used to follow us or not, and whether you knew. So many stories wander this roof – carefree, unrestrained – like Lalna!

❖

Are matters taking a serious turn? Until now, the conversations with Bitwa had taken place with me sitting like a statue and with my lips sealed. Now I've become animated. Life has crept unseen into that statue, and only now do I realize that my lips have started murmuring, my hands have started gesticulating!

Nevertheless, he sits facing away, himself a statue, unaware of Lalna.

What a grieving house you've left behind, Behen-ji!

But even in a house in mourning, the nature of conversations remains the same – starting at one place and ending up somewhere else. Yes, sir, we carry on endless conversations, Bitwa and I, even though that fool thinks he can become blind, deaf and dumb just by turning his back to me. He hears everything – what I say to him and even what I say to the maid. That's why I've received these comfortable, thick-soled Bata sandals today!

'Me and Behen-ji wore the same size – 5,' I had said to the maid.

That's why no one could tell who was on the roof with the doctor that day, near the jamun tree. Lalna's and Behen-ji's shoes, clothes, hair-clips, went from this body to that body – who could keep track?

Bitwa turns towards me in my imagination. Will he ask today what he could never bring himself to ask?

'Lalna.'

Oh, when he says my name, for a moment I'm overcome. Because he never really says it!

'Bitwa.'

'Who was upstairs?'

'Will you be able to handle the answer?'

'People say...'

'People are fools…'

'That two shadows were seen together every day.'

'They could have been anyone's shadows.'

'That Uncle used to follow them.'

'Om Babu never went to the roof.'

'Then how did your slippers and Chachcho's get lost, only to be found in his room?'

'The slippers got tired of waiting for us and came back!'

'That day, Uncle had the doctor's handkerchief.'

'So?'

'And…'

If he asks me today, will I tell him? Why? Let it be. The unfinished story of an unfinished life.

'A size-5 Bata sandal.'

'Whose?'

Mine or Behen-ji's? I laugh out loud. Come, Behen-ji, my heart yearns, let's laugh together.

He glares at me, suddenly aware of the possibility that it could've been Behen-ji. Oh, no, no, Bitwa, what are you thinking? That I want to slander your Chachcho? Whatever for? She had spread her wings and given me shelter. You're my friend, she said. Never mind if that loafer doesn't marry you, we're still friends. Forget that village, forget that deceitful man. No one's going to tell you now to don that veil, that wrap, that pallu. You're with me now. How can I slander that Behen-ji?

That Behen-ji. Who gave birth to you. Imbecile, do you think you'd have been able to come into this world if it weren't for her?

'Chachcho wasn't like that,' Bitwa stammers.

Like that? Spare her, why are you killing that poor dead woman all over again? Why do you want us friends to be invisible? How obsessed you people are with seeing us without our selves inside us!

❖

But there's no peace for Bitwa.

That's what a house in mourning is like – the living roam about like ghosts, in the house, on the roof, in solitude, hiding away from life.

That's how the people left behind after a loved one's death are – as if they too want to die!

The part of the roof he's staring at is being painted in preparation for Diwali.

Diwali shouldn't come after the rains. The whitewash spatters the trees and all the leaves become spotted, looking sick and pimply till the next rains.

We won't be able to celebrate Diwali. Otherwise I'd bring out Behen-ji's diamond set from the locker and wear it. But I will light a lamp, at least, at the window where our paths first crossed. For us, Lakshmi, Saraswati and even Durga came over the same path.

Where would Lalna be otherwise? The mere thought sends a shiver down my spine.

There's that house, which used to be Premanand-ji's. I can't remember anything when I look at it now. I don't want to remember anything.

The ways we come up with to erase bad memories – I once wanted to buy that house! 'Why?' Behen-ji was upset. 'To force your changed ways on that house?' She didn't let me buy it. As if, like the people of the mohalla, she was horrified by the thought of me being free and owning a house in their midst.

But her anxiety was different. For the first time, Lalna was making an independent decision. With her head in my lap, she cried, 'How young we were when we first met.' As if buying that house was the same as betraying her!

Behen-ji is dead.

Premanand-ji must also have gone and died somewhere. That house will also die. And when it has become a ruin, seedlings will burst out from its walls, peepal and banyan trees will grow. How many souls will roam its desolate roof? The ancestors will walk ahead, their heads shaking in arrogance, their fingers shaking in accusation. But Lalna will still be there, crying and laughing with all her heart, and going crazy with desire, so crazy that she won't even realize she's surrounded by a swarm of arid souls.

I look at Bitwa and scold him. Will you live your whole life without excitement? How can you love if you're such a pumpkin?

If you ask me, I will tell you that love isn't what you all think it is – man and woman and woman and man and bodies, bodies, bodies! Love affair, love affair! Lalna with Om Babu... Lalna with someone or the other... Lalna with that doctor... someone else with that doctor... If these are love affairs they're trifling, if they are the stuff of your imagination they're clichéd.

But when the darkness starts to sway with the gusts of wind, and when the sky starts turning around the axis of the roof, then no one can stop two friends, nothing can erase them. Our hearts jump into our mouths and a flame starts dancing in front of us and, to catch that flame bobbing like a balloon, we start moving with it.

Earth, fire, wind, water, space. Sometimes the five elements combine in such a way that they become the universe.

The two of us would go to the roof again and again. Not to meet anyone else, but to meet that flame. Sometimes in the scattered golden redness of the roof. Sometimes in the beautiful moonlight that looked like leaves scattered on the roof by the wind. Sometimes in the gradually fading green evenings of the roof.

The doctor didn't understand this. That we were making love to the wild winds, that he was blown in by chance, therefore some drops rained on him too.

He would come up to the roof after giving Om Babu his insulin injection and, hidden, he would listen to our songs.

❖

The rains had stopped that day.

We climbed up the stairs and opened the door to the roof.

Behind us everything was closed, the houses buried within the walls. In front of us was the open sky, and in the sky, shimmering red clouds.

We took off our slippers. When we lifted our feet to move forward, the creature inside us gave a little push, and as always we tipped ever so slightly ahead of the staid, familiar world, to some other world where every day some divine being was creating the sun for the first time and letting it shine, so that every particle could glimmer till late evening in that otherworldly light.

The people who came out onto that roof always seemed far away, like dark, magical shadows cast upon the shimmering curtain of the sky.

We would break into a song. Our voices would wander far and return, then disappear in the branches bent over the roof.

By chance, the doctor stood there, holding on to one such branch. By chance, he too fell under the spell of those tremulous melodies! And, by chance, he too was caught in those branches that we caressed with our voices and sometimes with our hands.

How were we to know? We'd sit on the parapet, swinging our legs, and when we couldn't stave off the thought of the two other creatures, their hunger and their sickness in the house down below, we'd go back.

Behen-ji's shawl slipped that day.

It fluttered down behind us to where the doctor stood rapt.

The doctor's head and Behen-ji's waist were at the same level. He picked up the shawl and gently pushed it into her lap.

Did she know? Did I know?

Why should I tell?

As it is, our songs and conversation were growing more and more seductive by the day.

We didn't even tell each other anything. But when, in the coming days, Behen-ji would feel warm breaths lightly blowing at her waist, she'd take my hand and place it there so that I could feel what she was feeling. And those warm breaths would start blowing on my arm as well.

❖

When Bitwa would ask us, 'Where were you,' Om Babu would squint and look around, then lick his finger to turn a page and start cutting something out from the magazine in hand, tracing a circle with a pair of scissors. But his ears would prick up.

The irony of it – when Behen-ji had wanted a husband,

Om Babu abandoned her and went off to make money. But when she rejected him, he closed up his business and started hanging around her like a pet dog! Yet he was never able to figure out how to reach her. She didn't fit in his frame any more. She had moved beyond what he could fathom and that left him feeling baffled and powerless.

Those terrible moments at night... When Behen-ji would thrash about like a caged animal. When he'd toss Behen-ji – who made him feel worthless in front of the whole mohalla, and even in front of this insignificant woman – aside like an irksome insect.

'Why did you go?' I'd cry out.

'He comes when he wants to, but when I...' Behen-ji looked so forlorn, as if she was waiting for something that, like a fever, was affecting her more and more every day.

Perhaps it's true, who knows, that a woman whose heart beats to a different tune loses her womanly charm. She bursts out of that form which is considered 'woman'. Looking at her, a man feels nothing. She provokes no love in his heart, nor desire in his body.

A woman who can't be fathomed is no woman!

'Where were you?' Bitwa would ask me.

I wouldn't answer, and he wouldn't wait for an answer either. Mostly, he'd leave me and go to Behen-ji.

He was growing up too. How could he not know what sort of respect to grant which woman?

'Do you see, Behen-ji?' Behen-ji would feel happy for herself and sad for me when I would ask her.

She'd say, 'It doesn't matter,' in the same voice in which she had once said of Premanand-ji's nephew, 'Forget that imbecile who doesn't want to marry you,' and hand me another cheque to deposit in my separate account.

Bitwa was suspicious.

'How did she manage to start a shop?' he would hesitantly ask Behen-ji and hurriedly walk away, as if that question was the end of the conversation.

By the time Om Babu had an inkling, I had already got Behen-ji to sign away their joint fixed deposits to me. Even she didn't know the full extent of it.

I did the right thing. So my life took off without anyone noticing. Would anything have come to me automatically? Would I have wandered around demanding my right? Fat chance of that. You have to take what you want. If you have to take leftovers, choose the best of those too. Don't beg for anything – not for relationships, not for food. How many more pieces can I break my heart into?

From the few remaining shares, Om Babu struck out Behen-ji's name. And he started adding Bitwa's name everywhere. He'd sit for hours, inspecting the papers in the trunk.

Once there was an earthquake in Laburnum House, rumbling and rattling. It seemed as if a group of trains was crashing through its walls. All the residents ran to their windows, as if there was someone out there who could stop the quake if they begged him to. Only Om Babu stood outside, carrying in his arms his trunk full of papers.

The earthquake stopped.

This too was Lalna's fault.

Just as much as Om Babu's coma.

❖

I heard something but couldn't understand what it was. There was no one near us on the roof. In the distance, even the air quivered like a shadow.

Later, people said they'd heard a loud crash. By the time we found out that the doctor's handkerchief and the size-5 Bata sandals had disappeared, it was too late and Om Babu was sleeping.

Om Babu!

Shouldn't I say his name the way we say the names of those who are no longer with us and then, looking into the distance, smile slightly – this slightness carrying a sense of all the pain in the world, all the sadness, the sourness, the cries, the pity, everything – and then tell the story of the one who is no longer with us?

So I say in that way: Om Babu.

And I smile in that elusive manner.

And now I'll tell you the story, remembering Om Babu, remembering my memories. Which tend to never begin at the beginning, but always start from somewhere in the middle.

His room was the sitting room. He and his trunk would be on the bed. A big armchair stood beside it. And near the armchair was the knobbed, wooden stand on which his hat and coat would hang, as if they could do nothing but hang after returning from Hong Kong.

Om Babu was lying there, fallen.

There was a loud crash on the roof. Who knows who heard it, but everyone began to say that he got a shock and fell, and it was his misfortune that he'd seen the doctor up there.

And it was his good fortune too, everyone said, that the doctor was up there and saw him.

The doctor said he'd fallen. Not on the roof, but in the sitting room. He laid him on the bed and inspected him for injuries.

'Om Babu, Om Babu,' he called.

'Open your eyes,' he ordered. 'Can you hear me?' he asked loudly.

First Om Babu's hand moved. Trembling, it reached for the trunk. Then his eyes opened.

'Are you all right?'

'What?'

'Why were you on the floor?'

'I was sleeping.'

The doctor turned to us. 'Has he eaten?'

'Yes,' I said.

His sugar levels were measured. 200. Not good at his age. The doctor advised stricter dietary restrictions.

Om Babu's eyes were closed, but he was saying that his head was aching, and one of his hands rested on the trunk while the other touched a corner of Behen-ji's sari, as if his whole world lay between these two things.

'He says his head is aching,' I said.

The doctor measured his pulse, placed a hand on his head, and called for Ibuprofen. The painkillers were forced down Om Babu's throat with two sips of water.

The doctor made a big mistake.

Om Babu slept all evening.

He slept all night.

He kept sleeping through the morning.

The tea went cold.

The food went cold. It was afternoon.

'How much will he sleep, Behen-ji?'

And then, all hell broke loose. Hospital. Tests. An internal head-injury. Did he hurt himself on the roof or in the sitting room?

The doctor had made a big mistake. He thought that Om Babu just needed to rest, that he would just sleep. Om Babu went into a deep, deep sleep and didn't wake up for the rest of his life.

As if instead of turning fifty, he'd turned eighty straightaway.

❖

When a respectable neighbour changes from a man to a vegetable, everyone wants to witness the wonder. With great difficulty, they stop their children from going to see the freak of nature and god and Lalna. You're too young, children!

But they come to the hospital. During visiting hours, and even afterwards. They barge into the room without even knocking, hoping to stumble upon some abject moment.

There's a tube in Om Babu's nose, there's a tube in his arm, there's a tube down his pyjamas. As if a heap of clothes has carelessly been strung up with ropes. The hospital bed is an iron cot, and the stands to the left and right of the bedhead are also made of iron. Big, fat bottles hang upside down from them, dripping glucose and medicine into Om Babu's body. The bag hanging below the cot is full of yellow urine.

In the middle of it all, Om Babu lies, alive yet lifeless.

People watch, horrified. The smell of urine and chloroform goes to their heads and makes them dizzy. They want to turn and leave the room and tell each other bluntly, see this is what happens, it would have been better if he'd died.

But before they can leave, they have to fulfil one important social duty, because the woman standing next to the vegetable is the vegetable's lawfully wedded wife. On her forehead is the honourable shadow of her sari's pallu – on her shoulders, the dust of a venerable relationship. They need to make her virtuousness even more virtuous.

The women of Laburnum House come and hug Behen-ji. 'Oh sister, how did this happen? What will you do now, you

poor thing? Where will you go? What a cruel joke. The pillar
that supported your home has fallen. It's only a husband
who can give a woman food, clothing and the protection of
his name. Oh sister, what a calamity has befallen you!'

'But don't cry, sister. You are lucky you're still unwidowed.
Whatever condition he's in, your husband's still with you.'
And they start weeping out of reverence.

Were they able to whisper that this is god's way of freeing
you from that other woman who had snared him with
her wiles? That now you can become the Savitri to your
Satyavan?

Men said in tearful voices, 'Such testing times, but you
will come through sister. Your strength and belief will carry
the day and stave off the worst.'

'You'll have to do everything yourself now,' people would
start saying as if they'd solved some difficult problem. 'Your
devotion will make him come back. Forget yourself. Don't
leave him alone for even one moment. And most certainly
not in someone else's care. You're simple, you trust easily.
The world is devious and selfish. Only you are truly there
for him.'

Before my very eyes, Behen-ji started retreating further and
further into herself. And on the outside, she became emptier
and emptier. Shining, bright, white, pure, shimmering.

Because too much light can also blind.

After everyone had left, the doctor started mumbling
again, 'I'm sorry, I'm sorry.'

The doctor had been careless, he had made a mistake.
By thinking that the coma was sleep. By looking outside for
injuries that were internal.

He offered a brilliant solution: He would get a private
room and a nurse for the comatose patient in the hospital.

He would bear all expenses. 'Sorry, I'm sorry,' he repeated. 'He will recover.'

Behen-ji looked at me, afraid.

'Take him home,' I said. 'I'm there, right?'

'Don't spare him, sister,' the worldly-wise neighbours said right in front of the doctor. 'We will take the matter to court.'

But the doctor had already started proceedings in the court of his soul. A regular supply of insulin, catheters, etc. started arriving every month, along with a wad of notes for the welfare of Om Babu's family. So that there would be no reduction in what Om Babu used to deposit every month on Behen-ji's table.

And there wasn't.

And Laburnum House was ecstatic. See? Her husband's still providing for her even though he's not conscious! And look at her: sorrowful, serving him, saint-like despite her age.

Behen-ji took all her colourful saris and glittering jewellery and handed them to me saying, here, take these Lalna, I won't wear them any more.

❖

Wind! Only you're here and no one else!

The conversation with Bitwa took such a turn that I completely forgot to see if he was near me or not, if he was still ignoring me, his back turned towards me.

But Bitwa went away, who knows when, and I sat here telling him all these things.

But no, not him – he shouldn't be told all this.

I lean forward to see if he's eaten the pancakes and the chilli pickle I sent. Of course he's eaten. How could he not?

He knows that my moves will always defeat him! Let him not eat. Then I'll draw myself up to my full stature and confront him saying, 'Why aren't you eating, you fool?' And he's not ready for that confrontation, so he quietly puts the food in his mouth.

One thing's for sure, Bitwa can't outmanoeuvre Lalna!

It's this fear that he has grown up with: Good god, who knows when she'll open her mouth! She might want to slap someone else, or she might think up some other mischief, and what if in the middle of all this she gets it into her head to spill my story?

Everyone wants to go abroad. But you, Bitwa, you didn't want to just go – you wanted to escape!

He comes out of the bathroom. It's me who quietly goes ahead of him and switches on the geyser. The weather's changing. We used to think Diwali fell in winter, but it's still warm. Still, there's no harm in being cautious.

He lies down. That's okay. Take a nap and talk to me after you wake up.

What will we talk about today?

Here, let me reassure you – don't be afraid, I'll never spill your secret. The hate peeking out from under your fear will keep my lips sealed. I've had enough of your accusations. As if I'd chosen to bear this son in my womb just so that I could deprive him of a respectable, well-known ancestry!

Neither you nor your Chachcho can understand the secrets of the womb. She also lived constantly in the fear that, seeing you draw closer and closer to her, I would speak out bluntly one day!

Listen both of you, if you can listen, this is the secret mantra of motherhood: a mother is not one whose womb pushes the baby out, a mother is one whose womb beckons it. See, if you can see: motherhood is a wave whose trajectory is not from the womb to the outside, but from the outside to the womb.

You are Behen-ji's son and no one else's.

Behen-ji, you are his mother, no one else.

Can you see, Behen-ji? Your son has stopped talking to me again. Like the time when Om Babu was in a coma. But I still keep talking to him.

'What was it called, Bitwa?'

He's asleep, but it seems to me that he has woken up at my words!

'What are you asking?'

'What was it that the doctor used to measure?'

'Lalna,' he scolds.

I like it! 'Yes, Bitwa?'

'Don't pretend to be ignorant.'

'But I don't remember,' I whimper.

'Liar.'

'Yes.'

'Tell the truth.'

'Take my name again.'

'Lalna. Now tell me.'

'What?'

'What was it that the doctor used to measure?'

'GCS score.'

'Yes.' He's playing the teacher! 'Which stands for?'

'Glasgow Coma Scale.'

'You know everything.'

'Yes.'

No, Bitwa will say, 'You know everything, Lalna.' He will definitely say 'Lalna'.

We both laugh.

It looks like he's fast asleep. Who knows what he's buried away in his heart?

And here I am, sitting in the verandah and talking to that sleeping statue.

Nothing happens for the first time in a house in mourning. Before me, it was Behen-ji who would drag a stool to sit at Om Babu's side so that she could talk to him like this, alone.

❖

I would mop his room with phenyl, not the maid.

Early in the morning, Behen-ji would bathe, get ready and come stand at the door. Long before treacherously dying in my absence.

There was a slight nip in the air, like today.

Behen-ji removes her slippers and enters the room, stands beside the bed, staring at Om Babu who looks like a statue made of ash. She leans forward and curls her lips as if she's about to blow on that statue to see whether the ash will fly.

'He's stinking,' she says and turns around to open the window.

The golden rays of the morning sun dance upon Om Babu.

I close the window. 'Wait,' I scold her.

Behen-ji pulls up a stool and sits, and her lips begin to move as she starts talking to Om Babu.

I help him sit up, piling up pillows against the wall for him to lean back on. His eyes are closed, his head lolls.

Unbuttoning his shirt, I turn him to one side. His head lolls. I pull the shirt off one arm and then turn the other shoulder to get the other sleeve. His head lolls to that side.

I can hear the sound of his long, ragged breaths as he exhales through his nose.

I turn the naked statue of ash this way and that, and clean carefully. Whatever's supposed to support the neck and head seems to have snapped. The slightest nudge and his head swings here or falls there.

I wet some soap for shaving and work up a lather.

'Keep his head straight,' Behen-ji scolds me. She doesn't like the lolling head. 'It looks like he's been hanged.'

Suddenly, she starts laughing.

Om Babu lies there, eyes closed. When his GCS score dropped from nine to four or five, the doctor let us bring him home. Who knows, now he might just wake up.

Behen-ji cuts her laughter short and asks, 'Do you think he can hear us?'

I'm moving the razor above his chapped lips.

'Cut him,' Behen-ji says. 'Let's see if it hurts.' She becomes greedier, 'Will he bleed?' She presses down on my hand which holds the blade. Om Babu's head slips and falls to one side. Drool trickles out of his mouth.

'Wipe it, wipe it.' Behen-ji steps back.

I wipe it. I stick the corner of a handkerchief into his eyes to clean the gunk. Then I wipe his naked body clean with a wet towel. This way and that, gingerly.

The ashen statue stays ashen.

When I change the sheet, Behen-ji turns away at the sight of shit stains. Although she does hold a corner of the clean sheet to help make the bed.

I dress Om Babu in a clean kurta and lay him down again, but he doesn't open his eyes. Behen-ji leans over him and pushes his eyelids open with her fingers. The eyes are still there, living but dead, unseeing.

I turn around on hearing her make some sound. Foo... foo... foo... She's blowing upon those stony eyes.

Her fingers hold them firmly open and she blows, sometimes on the right eye, sometimes on the left, so hard that a shower of spit shimmers in the sunlight.

'Enough,' I say. 'Bitwa is coming.'

❖

Oh, but where? Bitwa isn't coming anywhere! And I don't want to talk about these things with him, even if he wants to. These memories just came along on their own as I sat alone, remembering. There's nothing for you in all this, Bitwa. You are far from the heart of this matter.

The beating heart of it lies in someone else, where the slightest whisper can rise and slowly turn into a tumultuous din that surrounds the two girls who grew up together and were together as children and old women, yet those who saw them together would never know that they were together.

'True or false?' I ask Bitwa, not caring about where he is right now. He stares at me in surprise.

'Did you see what everyone saw?'

'Yes, I saw.'

Should I make a face? You know everything, you've seen everything!

'Tell me.'

'Chachcho would sit next to Uncle all the time.'

I'm not saying this, he is. And everyone else.

'As if meditating.'

'Her lips moving lightly, her fingers waving in the air, her eyes opening and closing.' I am saying this. I have seen it.

'As if praying.' Bitwa speaks.

'Tell me more.'

'She used to wear a white sari.'

'Not white, but plain, yes.'

'She started covering herself up.'

'She did. But later.'

'She stopped going to the roof.'

'She did. But later.'

'Her hair turned white.'

'They didn't, but that's what everyone claims.'

'If people came to visit, they'd beat a hasty retreat.'

'So that they didn't disturb her prayers.'

Did I say that, or Bitwa?

The ability to put scene and dialogue in the correct order seems to have deserted me. Perhaps it's because of the changing weather. It's still warm, but winter's well on its way.

I start to stand up. To do that, I have to first press my hands against the armrests and support myself. I've become fat and old.

Already?

Behen-ji, the plaster in your room is peeling. We'll get it scraped and mended and painted next year. And since you are no more, why not hang a big picture of you as well?

Standing on my feet, I choose a place on the wall above Behen-ji's desk. I stretch out my arm as if there's a spring in it and point, 'Here…'

Slowly, I let my arm return to my body.

Why does my heart feel so full and my body so empty?

Unhurriedly, I lean against the window in the room.

How often Behen-ji must have stood like this when she stopped going to the roof after my departure. Covered from head to toe, withdrawn, almost invisible. Had I passed by and looked up from the street, I would only have seen a blurred, cloaked form there. When the slightest touch of breeze would move her hand to a corner of the window, I would think a shadow had moved. Moving towards her death as if in a dream, or a nightmare?

Look, the window is turning into a pair of supple arms and leaning over me...

❖

There's a fire smouldering in my heart. I want to save and pluck out the half-burnt remains from it. What are they? I can't recognize them. They're all the shape of ash, the colour of ash.

Defeated, I let it be. I don't put my hand in the burning flames.

Someone's checking my pulse. Must be a doctor.

Not *that* doctor, Bitwa! Who used to send little swirls of air tumbling on our skin.

'Fever... Blood pressure...' These words fall on my ears.

I want to open my eyes. Who's speaking? To whom? Are my eyes open? Who's in front of me? Behen-ji?

She on that side of the bed, me on this side.

Flickering fire. Ah ha ha ha! Such fun! Every bit of my body feels so hot that it might turn into vapour and disappear at a touch. Where's the pain hidden in all this fever?

In the middle, a lifeless body on the bed.

Mine? Om Babu's.

What is Behen-ji saying?

'Blow, blow,' Behen-ji hisses.

We blow. To bring his body to life, or ours? Oh, who's moved the sheet off Om Babu? Raising his kurta, we blow on his chest. On his shoulder. On his feet. On his thighs. On his eyes.

Foo… foo… foo…

Embers tumble down my body. Burning embers so tiny that they've become damp from the blowing – by Behen-ji?

Ah ha ha ha, how it hurts. Somewhere. Where? Pain rustles up and down my skin.

Like witches, we keep blowing, foo… foo… foo… on Om Babu. Hot air. Burning air.

A hand on my forehead.

Behen-ji… Oh Behen-ji…

I can't sleep… Me neither… Shall we go… Let's go… Shall we run… Let's run… On the roof… Leaving him to die here… Don't worry… Someone will see… Afraid again… No one sees you… Even when they see you they don't see you…

Behen-ji comes and sits by my side, shaped like a shadow.

Stop hiding now, what are you afraid of?

Oh Ma, how it hurts. I want to dance like a lunatic!

Whispers, murmurs fall on my ears from afar.

What are you saying, Behen-ji?

…

What did you give me to drink, Behen-ji?

…

How long have I been sleeping?

…

Now you're asleep and I'm asleep!

…

Oh, you're still sitting by my bedside? Let me look at you a moment. Haven't seen you in ages. Have you also become invisible ever since you died?

Was that Bitwa?

Forget him.

Hadn't I already forgotten him long ago? Forget them before they forget you!

What are these voices sounding inside me? As if big blocks of wood are falling heavily into the fire within me.

Ball… Slipper… Mortar… Pestle… Engine… Plate… Caw, Caw… Bang… Whirr… Bam.

Lalna's world is burning and you're all bent on grinding and pounding?

Who are all these people milling around my bed?

Om Babu was on the bed. How did I fall into it?

Behen-ji. Bitwa.

Where is everyone?

Have my eyes opened?

No Bitwa… No Behen-ji…

Just a table. And Lord Krishna lounging on a book with his toe in his mouth.

No, no. Behen-ji had never used Krishna as a, what's it called, paperweight. The book to one side. Krishna resplendent on another.

Easy now… Don't fall… Looks like you need a cane now.

Krishna, get away from the book and suck at your toe. Gloriously!

There's a tremor in my feet. Easy now… No other safe place except for the bed.

Should I sleep, then?

Good that I moved Krishna off the book and kept him in his proper place. Like Behen-ji used to.

I'm the one who knows Behen-ji, not you! What place do you have in our friendship?

❖

If I close my eyes, Behen-ji and I are skipping rope.

One, two… fifty-five, fifty-six…

There's excitement in the air… Whoosh goes the rope through the air… Whoosh we jump… Whoosh under our feet… Whoosh our roof!

Breathlessness can be such fun!

We skip on and on, going higher and higher, with every breath, rising a little above the roof, one breath above the roof, one breath closer to the sky!

The doctor forces my eyes open and peers in. Stranger.

'You people don't even let me jump,' I mumble.

'How is she?' Bitwa asks the doctor.

'I'm perfectly fine,' I answer him directly, dismissing the doctor, and behind closed eyes I start skipping with Behen-ji once more. How high above the roof our rope soars!

Whoosh… whoosh!

Behen-ji's hair, tied up in a bun, starts to unravel.

'Times,' she says and sets her hair loose.

And then we start again!

One… two… and a hundred and one!

Sparks scatter inside my head because of the fireworks.

'Drink this medicine.'

Do not disturb… Whoosh… Jump…

Now many hands prise my jaw open!

'I'm all right now,' I say through the bitterness pouring into my mouth.

I won't open my eyes.

Not me, nor Behen-ji! Whenever we open our eyes, people meet our gaze and create someone else in our stead. So we've closed our eyes, ignoring them.

When we close our eyes, we skip rope. We're panting, but we don't let the rope tangle with our feet.

Who... who... whoosh... We jump, the rope swings. With springs in our legs and a spindle in the rope, we swing and the rope jumps.

Then the rope starts skipping us! We sail through the air, round and round, and the rope jumps to avoid us!

One... two... three... a hundred and four...

'Tea.'

Bitwa's voice.

Toast and tea before my eyes.

I look askance at Behen-ji's desk and my suspicions are confirmed – Krishna is lying on the book again.

Behen-ji never did that. I pick up the cup grumpily and my hands tremble.

When I sit up, the room spins. I close my eyes tight. One... two... three... There we go skipping again. And that's how, sailing through the air, I reach the desk!

Krishna goes off the book. He lies separately. The book lies on the other side. As it used to be when Behen-ji was around.

Eyes closed. Skipping... dancing with the wind...

And I crash into the pillow!

'The doctor's said you must eat toast.' A scolding voice. An unseen presence. Bitwa's.

Have you gone and died too? A laugh wants to burst out and splash around in the teacup. Then, suddenly on one side, a splashing, swaying image appears – Bitwa's – and disappears. Or is it my eyes that are causing the swaying and splashing?

I dip the toast in tea and gulp it down.

When I close my eyes again, the rope and I automatically start our skipping game in order to not crash into each other.

Fast

Fast

Then less

And less

Now slow

Slow

Very slow

Almost at rest

The rope held in both hands, its looped end licking my feet like a pet dog.

Krishna on the table…

What? He's on the book again?

Behen-ji didn't keep him there, I want to scream, but the words lie defeated in my weary heart. And now I'm slipping into a deep sleep…

❖

Someone kept coming to the room in those days of fever, when I'd go off to skip rope with Behen-ji behind closed eyelids, to move Krishna from his place on the table and keep him on the book. Which I couldn't allow because I knew that Behen-ji never kept him like that.

I'd set it right and he'd spoil it again.

And in doing so, he'd remove Behen-ji from her own memory.

Rascal, rogue! Would I now have to concede defeat to someone whose shit and piss I had cleaned?

He'd move Krishna and leave medicines and some food for me.

Khichdi.

So I have another plan. You've moved Krishna. All right,

I won't move him back to Behen-ji's preferred place. But I won't eat the khichdi either!

Not that this khichdi is edible anyway. I never served such horrid, watery khichdi to Om Babu even. And remember, even if Behen-ji didn't want to – she felt this boiled mash was good enough – I'd still give him a spoonful or two of kheer, or crumbs of his favourite kachori, or nibbles of the little pakoris we used for curry.

I would feed him with my hands, I didn't sneak in, leave the food and sneak back out like this. Holding his head in these very hands, I would make him sit back and spoon the food little by little into his mouth, the way one fills a narrow-mouthed bottle without spilling anything. A bit might trickle out, but a bit goes in too. And if Om Babu couldn't eat even then, well, it was just his luck gone to ashes!

When I'd lay his head back on the pillow after feeding him, I could even see a very faint, lopsided smile forming on his lips.

'Look Behen-ji, he seems satisfied.'

'And why not,' Behen-ji would rage, 'since he's tied me down once more.'

At which Om Babu broke wind.

How startled we were! That peaceful, quiet statue made of ash, his eyes closed, his limbs powerless. Fate had delivered him into these hands. We could lift and drop him, twist and break him if we wanted and he couldn't do a thing. He was living on our pity. But had he managed to keep his soul from us? Where we couldn't reach it? A secret life, a secret pulse somewhere deep inside him… And at its direction – wind!

Oh Ma! Scared, I move my head this way and that on the pillow. Have I also turned into a statue of ash?

I have to ask Bitwa what happened. Yes, I know I had

fever, but was I up there or somewhere down below, diving, sinking to the bottom? Everyone shouted Mister Om, Mister Om… No, I mean, Lalna, Lalna… Open your eyes… Who am I? Can you recognize me… How many fingers am I holding up… Who are you… What's your name?

What answers did I give? Did I say something in Chinese? Like Om Babu?

Open your mouth… Stick your tongue out…

Oh Ma! And did I also lie prone and lifeless, struggling to stick my tongue out as if it were deep inside my mouth, so that it peeped out and quickly went back in like a snake in its hole? How laughable!

And did I also… wet… the bed… sometimes… Oh dear… And who cleaned me?

How can I ask Bitwa all this?

I lie quietly. Looking around with a detached expression.

And then I see the table, and my eyes stop moving. What's this? Krishna isn't sitting on the book today!

I start eating the khichdi. And I start to wonder whether I should respond to this peace-offering by going and placing Krishna on the book myself, as a favour.

❖

'How are you feeling, Madam?' the maid stands in attendance with soup and bread.

'My mouth tastes bitter.' I pull a face.

Amazing! The fever seems to have increased people's regard for me.

'It's because of the medicine,' the maid explains.

'Throw it all away,' I say angrily.

'Sir is watching,' she softly warns me.

At the mention of 'Sir', I steal a glance at Krishna. He's still in the correct place. I've won!

Or have I actually lost? Did he concede defeat for my sake? And will I win only if I counter this move as well? By making Krishna lie down on the book like a paperweight for his sake?

But all the strength in my body seems to have deserted me.

Some regret sneaks into my heart – if I hadn't recovered, the games that we'd started playing while I'd been unconscious with fever wouldn't have stopped. Stumbling over to the table thinking, I won't fall now, I'll fall some other time, and swaying while keeping the statue in its proper place, then coming to and looking expectantly in that direction, hoping that the contest was still on, daring myself to make a move, which would give my ailing heart a new, bracing energy.

Oh the ecstasy of illness! As soon as I closed my eyes, I'd start skipping rope with Behen-ji and could feel that someone had quietly come to sit by me. No, he couldn't have seen us skipping. He must have thought I was unconscious.

Perhaps someone is silently skipping behind every unconsciousness. Om Babu must have been travelling around the universe, skipping a rope all those years, while Behen-ji, sitting beside him still as a statue, thought he was in a coma.

Maybe he could hear her when she softly told him everything.

'Look, Lalna. He's not smiling now,' she'd say. 'He didn't like what I said.'

What? Did he just mumble some gibberish? I would bend over Om Babu's face. I never thought I'd ever be able to go so close to this person and he wouldn't be able to push me away.

As his stale smell would reach me, I'd look at Behen-ji with a sort of thrill.

I'd lean over this side of Om Babu. She'd stand on that side of Om Babu. As if taking positions to start a new game.

'What's the programme?' Behen-ji would look at me with a mischievous glint in her eyes.

'Om Babu, are you with or against our programme?' I'd whisper as if in a trance.

'He stopped us from going to the roof,' Behen-ji would hiss from between her teeth.

We would reach out to each other over Om Babu.

'What is it?'

'A beehive.'

Our hands, forming a circle above him, would fill with elation.

'How many honeybees are there?'

'Thousands upon thousands.'

'Making honey.'

'But diabetics won't get any.'

We'd make a hive over Om Babu, which contained a million honeybees – buzzing, their many melodies merging into one – and their sticky, humming liveliness. Under it, Om Babu would lie lifeless, yet listening to everything, knowing that this ball of fire was hovering just above him.

'Don't even try to wake up,' Behen-ji softly said.

'You will be stung and burnt,' I said.

And as in countless other programmes, we started singing this time too, as if giving our every breath its due.

When, hand in hand, we'd enjoy our programme everything would be in the throes of romance!

And sometimes under our faces, we'd feel Om Babu's lifeless breath tremble, as if our song had tickled his stillness, had shaken it.

❖

'I will take a proper bath today.' I tell the maid who has come to sponge me to take away the bucket of water, the towel and the powder. 'Now you can go.'

Bitwa has gone to office. Today this house seems stranded between the departing summer and the arriving winter.

I wander alone through the house. From my room to the sitting room, from the sitting room to the room near the courtyard, to Bitwa's room on the other side of the courtyard. In the courtyard. In the verandah. If I look towards the trellis, the upstairs rooms are visible. The sunlight coming through it brings the shapes of the roof down to me in the form of huge shadows.

There's silence all around. With the fever gone, the footsteps also seem to have gone from the house. Yes, there is in the distance the infinitely mundane clatter of Laburnum House.

It feels good, the emptiness. The watery sunlight. The absence of anyone else. The ceasing of footsteps.

I leave the bathroom door open. The commode is cold.

When it starts becoming warm, I get up for a minute. When the cold settles on it once more, I will let it touch my skin again.

There's some ancient coconut oil here. I splash it on my body and massage it in. Massage it, to push my body into the shape it once used to be. I move fistfuls of flesh from here to there. From down to up. From outside to inside. This flesh that's sopping with oil, I gather and fold. My arms start to tire from massaging myself. Each arm holds the other to assuage their mutual pain.

Oh, won't someone fill up a big drum with water from the tank. Then we can go to the roof and sit under the stars. Water that has cooled under the moon is something else. It's as if you're bathing with moonlight.

Like water heated under the sun. Then you bathe with sunlight!

I sit on a stool, holding on to the tap, and rest my head on my tired arms. The bucket is full to the brim. I'm so tired that even a little mug full of water seems heavy. Slowly, I pour it over myself with a tired pleasure.

So pleasurable is the exhaustion that I wrap a towel without drying myself and sit back down on the stool.

A cold wind is coming through the door. I should get up. Tap, help me stand. Door, hold my hand. Wall, lend me a shoulder.

I stagger out with the towel around me. Will I fall? Who says I'll fall? See, I've come into the verandah. See, I'm leaning against a pillar. The bed has gone from the room by the courtyard. Come, keep walking and go straight to Behen-ji's room. Our room. My room.

A pang of sorrow in my heart. I stop at the window.

My body has dried, it feels heavy under the towel. Behind leaden eyelids, my soul has become more and more alone. Something else should have happened, something else could have happened – my loneliness cries.

Behen-ji and I look at each other. With so much sadness.

Strange, I'm standing right where she used to stand. Suddenly I'm frightened by the thought that the dry earth I'm standing on right now was once a rolling sea. What if a whirlpool or a sea snake is still around? Or if the sea turns back and floods this place again? That's how tides work, isn't it? They ebb and flow...

Did I just rock like a boat? I'm sinking into sleep.

I let myself fall into Behen-ji's chair. The towel goes here, I go there.

There's a warmth in the cushioned chair that touches my cold body. As if Behen-ji had been sitting here all this while and just stood up, so that I could sit in her afterglow.

❖

That's what friends do.

They recognize each other's afterglow, and when they see each other losing it, they laugh a spiteful laugh.

When Bitwa used to come home from college, Behen-ji would watch as I ran to open the door for him. Seeing her smile scornfully, I'd want to stop and give her a tight slap, but the velocity of my legs wouldn't permit it.

The moment between running quickly to the door and halting completely to open it is a confused moment, suspended between speed and slowness. Which has stopped in one place for eternity, which is constantly teetering on the edge, which is silently throbbing.

The same thing happens over and over again: I keep opening the door, I keep finding Bitwa in front of me... I keep opening the door, holding back my emotions... And behind me, every time, Behen-ji's laughter, which only a friend can hear, cruel yet compassionate.

My son would greet me half-heartedly and quickly go to Behen-ji. Then it would be my turn to look at her kindly and laugh scornfully.

He's in Om Babu's room with Behen-ji, making sure his

Uncle's being taken care of properly, flaunting his newly acquired sense of responsibility.

'Did you measure his blood sugar today...? Fasting sugar...? And after his meal...?'

I'm on the other side of the door. From here, I can see the soles of Om Babu's feet. He's lying with his feet sticking out from under the sheet. And they're festering with awful cracks!

Quickly, I get to work. Heading in with soap and a bucket full of water.

I move Om Babu so that his legs dangle from the bed and I can soak his feet in soapy water. Then, taking a pumice stone, I scrub his heels, making them soft and smooth like a baby's. With a brush, I scour his nails and clean the dirt from under them. His toe hairs are so long, they could get tangled in the brush. Scrub, scrub, clean, clean.

I dry his feet, apply cream on them, and tuck them back in, when my heart is overcome with tenderness. As if they're two scared little rabbits, peeking out from under the sheet.

There, there, I try to reassure them, before I notice that Behen-ji and Bitwa are still standing at the window, talking.

What are they talking about? I turn my head in order to listen better, but Bitwa falls silent.

'Shall we go?' Behen-ji says. Brushing lightly against me as she leaves, to let me know that she's the winner.

Now they are outside and I am inside.

I keep sitting on the stool with my bucket and brush and pumice stone, and Om Babu keeps lying in front of me. At this angle, his nostrils look like big tunnels. The hair inside has turned white.

Oh Ma! Did you see? I have to tell Behen-ji!

❖

Bitwa is scolding the maid: Why did you leave her alone, why did you let her bathe, do I have nothing better to do than to set aside all my work and stand guard here?

My back hurts from lying too long on one side. But I can't turn by myself. Forget turning, I can't even open my eyes by myself!

What's this sickness that has gripped you all, making you confine me to the bed again and again? But then you can't just lay me down and disappear. Remember your Uncle at least.

I used to examine him every day. Only once did he get a boil that had suppurated before we found out. Oh, it must have hurt! And he couldn't even tell us. After that, I'd run my hand all over his body every now and then. I'd hold him and make him work out.

Like your Chachcho made you do, Bitwa, when you were a baby.

Arms straight, close to the body, arms straight, away from the body. One leg up, one leg down. The other leg up, the other leg down. Then I'd roll Om Babu over this side and that. I'd dust him with boric powder to prevent boils and rashes. I'd move his muscles so that they didn't start atrophying, and Om Babu could get up and march like a soldier, left-right, left-right, whenever he chose!

Aren't they afraid that if they leave me lying like this then tomorrow, when I want to get up, I'll have forgotten how to move my hands and feet?

What… What is he saying?

The doctor's searching for my pulse. He can't find it! Did you bribe someone for your degree? Try harder, it has to be somewhere!

Is that you, Bitwa?

Let me see… I can't see…

He must be scared. That he'll have to deal with another death! But why would I come here to die? There's a whole wide world out there where I could go to kick the bucket.

No, don't be scared. Why would I die? I've just fallen ill, that's all. The fever that didn't come all these years has finally arrived, with a vengeance, perhaps.

Or is it an ingenious ploy to stay longer? So that I can fleece you some more?

Say it: Behen-ji's indulged me far too much!

'Hey, where's the change we got from the newspaper man... hey this... hey that...'

Is that an accusation I'd even respond to?

But Behen-ji – 'Lalna!'

What is this Lalna-Lalna? It had been lying around for so many days, the maid or anyone else could have pocketed it and you wouldn't even know. But if Lalna puts it away in her purse, all hell breaks loose!

Why would you associate me with theft?

But it's all right. Everything is all right. These old matters, they're remembered and forgotten. Those who had to die have died. Those who have to live, no one can kill.

No, I'm not dying. I just feel sleepy.

Yes, I should sleep.

❖

I wake up as if from a long sleep.

Like Behen-ji. Will you ever wake up?

Like Om Babu would surely wake up one day, the people of Laburnum House believed, when Behen-ji's penance would vanquish death.

It feels good to have slept, as if making up for all the sleep that I'd lost. A peaceful yawn gathers inside me, and I stretch languidly.

Bitwa turns. Our eyes meet and a recognition passes between us. Then he turns away without batting an eyelid.

Towards the TV. It seems that, while I slept, he brought it out of his room and installed it here, and sat himself down in front of it. Beside me!

There's news on the TV, but I can't hear it. And from outside, the night seeps in and roams the house in search of light.

The TV is in front of us, facing us both. Bitwa's chair is some yards away with its back towards my bed, so that he can't see me unless he turns. But he isn't hiding. Instead, and this thought makes me smile, he is clearly watching over me.

I take a pillow and set it against the bedhead, raise my head a little, and start watching TV.

While I was resting, Bitwa rested too. I moved a little and now he has become watchful. Well, I have a body, which means I sometimes have to use the bathroom, and when I get up to go to the bathroom, he gets up too, alert.

Returning to the room, I pick up the food he's served for me in the meantime. Chapattis with ghee, daal, peas, cauliflower, salad. I start eating.

He starts eating too. With his back to me, watching TV.

Some energy seems to have started flowing in me. My blood pressure must have improved. Where's the doctor – tell him to examine me carefully now. Is the blood pressure still low? Anaemia?

Shameless creature, I curse myself. All this rude health is only for show – inside you're still weak and hollow.

Should I ask Bitwa?

But I keep eating alone.

It doesn't work like this. My coming here and falling sick, his sitting by my side – it doesn't resolve everything that has remained unresolved between us. Unresolved things tend to stay unresolved, that's their nature. They just roll and churn inside us. Do you know how many lives have passed, how many centuries have passed, how many things remain unspoken?

Let it be! Can this old crone turn into the young Lalna from a thousand years ago? Just let me get the strength to walk once more, so that I don't lie curled up all day, so that I don't have to give up going to the roof – that's all I want.

When I move to keep the plate, Bitwa starts to get up. He's scared – sometimes I fall, sometimes my towel falls!

I'm feeling sleepy again. It's all nicely lined up – the TV, Bitwa and me, sleeping and waking, sleeping and waking.

Before falling asleep, I catch sight of the trunk under the TV. Om Babu's trunk! When we broke the lock, his treasure came to light – share certificates, account books, size-5 Bata sandals, a man's handkerchief, and clippings of matrimonial ads for fair, homely, beautiful, vegetarian, convent-educated girls pinned to Om Babu's bio-data. As if the trunk was not a trunk but the hidden darkness of Om Babu's heart, from which Behen-ji had managed to ferret out the cursed fragments of his desires.

❖

We've started eating together while watching TV, although we still pretend to not see each other.

And silently.

The fever hasn't returned. I'm slowly regaining my strength.

The low hum of the TV is great for falling asleep. I sleep well and wake up silently.

No, I don't scream. I won't scream.

That scream was so loud, you could hear it on the roof. As if, rising from the foundations of the house and tearing through the ceiling, it wanted to reach the sky. I ran downstairs.

'Behen-ji, Behen-ji…'

She sat unfazed on the stool, as if deep in thought.

'Did he scream? He screamed, didn't he?'

'Are you sure?' The doctor was right there. 'He screamed? Om Babu, Om Babu, can you hear me?' he shouted.

In the doctor's eyes, an astonishing happiness – the stain on his conscience might yet be erased! Would Om Babu wake up? He stared, as if he really could raise the dead. He took his torch and shone it in Om Babu's eyes, hoping to get some reaction.

Behen-ji's face was red with rage. As if she knew this would give rise to some new excuse to tie her down. Why did you scream for no rhyme or reason? You're sleeping comfortably and we're doing everything for you, then why…?

'We must take him to the hospital.' The doctor was looking even younger now. 'We'll have to measure his GCS score again.' He looked happily towards Behen-ji, yet it was as if he'd flooded the room with unhappiness.

Love. The love of girls. The love of women.

Love, that always remains incomplete, unspoken, unlived…

Earth, fire, wind, water, space. When the five elements combine, they create love. For a moment.

Then those who are in love move towards each other. What permutations and combinations flutter in the air?

No, nothing of that sort happens. When love brings you face to face, really close, it turns into an immense sadness. Then you see each other really close, face to face, but you don't touch each other, you can't touch each other.

The doctor was injecting something, Bitwa was making a list, Behen-ji was adjusting the pallu on her head, the residents of Laburnum House were whispering, Om Babu was either conscious or unconscious and lay convulsing, Lalna was cleaning him up and getting him ready – every one of them was staring, and who can tell who was seeing whom really close, but didn't touch, couldn't touch…

Oh, how I cried when I saw my two rabbits! What a state they must have been in to be twitching so! And would they return safely? Would they return at all? If they returned, wouldn't they be grubby? If they returned, would they still find me here, unchanged?

It was as if a bridal procession was leaving this house, my rabbits slowly slipping out of my hands!

It broke the hearts of the residents of Laburnum House. Later, they would say that when Om Babu was being taken to the hospital, his wife fell at his feet and burst into tears.

❖

Bitwa is quietly watching TV.

So am I. Quietly, reclining on the bed.

If you stay where you belong, people respect you. But if you try to move out of that pigeonhole, it makes them uneasy.

I move. I sit up and put my slippers on. Good, very good, I don't feel dizzy at all.

I stand.

'I'll go to the roof for a bit,' I say loudly.

He looks at me strangely. He'll come after me, so that I see him but don't think that he's keeping a watch on me, so that if some mischief occurs to me I'll realize that he's there, keeping a watch on me.

It rained last night. Waves of darkness roll through the dusky hues of the roof. Layers of dust have congealed and become slippery, like moss.

Someone's charpoy is lying on the roof. A couple of labourers squat beside it, vigorously restringing it.

Even today you can see charpoys in Laburnum House. This must be a matter of disposition.

It's said that we all are born with some sort of disposition. The people of Laburnum House are disposed to tossing nuggets of gossip around on the roof. So Lalna is disposed to catching hold of those nuggets and playing marbles with them! My heart starts singing at the thought. The excitement of tossing fistfuls of marbles on the roof and hearing them clatter as they scatter all around.

Wherever she goes, she'll cause ruin – a matter of disposition. Who knows how many she's ruined in her village. And here, Premanand-ji and his family, Uncle, Chachcho, the nephew…

The way the scorpion stung the tortoise who saved him from the flood – a matter of disposition.

And when there's no one left, will Lalna sting herself?

Behen-ji, should she be killed or should she be spared? Come one, come all and bring your ancestors to this deposition of dispositions. Lalna will sit in judgement. Whoever apologizes to her will be forgiven. Those who don't will be ruined.

No one's ever apologized to Lalna. Apologize. You must apologize!

Did my body suddenly slip out of Behen-ji's phulkari shawl, is that why it fluttered away and fell in a heap?

The cold touch of the roof on my cheek.

Why are you carrying me? Let me lie there a while. So that, when I stand up, my shape remains imprinted in the dust.

You let Om Babu lie for years, give me at least a moment!

All right, all right, I'm not going to protest like him. He couldn't see, he couldn't walk, but with every ragged breath that vegetable only begged to live. Those comatose breaths didn't demand to get up or run on the roof or swim in its air. They only said, don't let me stop breathing – let one breath come, let one breath go, let me exist, that's enough, whether I know it or not, let me just be, that's enough!

'Lalna,' Behen-ji's fervent voice asked, 'he's not dying, is he?'

A stampede in his lungs answered, I'm not dying, am I? Do something. Don't let me go.

Behen-ji's panic-stricken face.

Om Babu on an artificial respirator. The vegetable has lost its sweetness, its ripeness, its greenness, but it won't dry up and fall from the tree. What do they say? Keep it safe in the greenhouse!

And my rabbits are going from white to black, becoming grimy, grubby.

'Let him go,' the doctor said.

Behen-ji's eyes searched for me.

Yes, it was Lalna who went into that hospital ward which smelled of anaesthetic, where Om Babu was counting his last breaths – one, two, three… With the doctor. Pull the tube. Disconnect him from life.

He was alive when she went in, people said, when she came out he wasn't.

I hear the song of a cuckoo.

A cuckoo? In this season?

❖

I think aloud: 'In my time she used to sing during the rains, hidden behind leaves.'

Then once more there's silence between us.

We're climbing down the stairs that will lead to the courtyard.

When we reach the courtyard, I jerk away from Bitwa's arm.

'Not she, he,' he suddenly says. And continues, 'Where are there leaves for him to hide now? You can see him clearly.'

'The cuckoo? You can see her? I've never seen one. I've just heard the song. And I know that she's black.'

I sit in bed, all wrapped up in sheets, feeling elated.

'He's black,' Bitwa says. 'Eyes, red and angry like a drunkard's. Beak, yellow.'

He, not she, he said.

I should keep quiet now, satisfied that he has spoken even this much. What if I say something and he clams up again? But I can't help it.

'But you can see her? Amazing!'

'I can see *him*. *He* is black. You can see the female too, but she's not black. She's brown, with white spots or stripes or some such pattern.'

'Then take me there. I want to see her from up close...'

But I know he won't take me there, this son of mine who sits watching TV with his back to me. With my fever gone, his fever will return. And then he'll look at me with contempt once more. He'll think that I broke his dreams, that I soured his happiness. As if he'd even have existed without me, as if he'd have sprung from some respectable family, as if he'd have a better disposition!

These words roll inside me like thunderclouds.

They emerge not from my lips but from my eyes, frightening him into a nervous stutter: 'El Niño... La Niña... Nature's clock has been messed up... Unseasonal rain... Hot in winter, cold in summer... And with the seasons lost, the cuckoo too has lost his mind... Doesn't sing when he's supposed to, doesn't stay quiet when he's supposed to...'

'What?' I look outside the window. The branch of the neem tree is an arm's length away. Does the cuckoo sit on this?

Sitting in bed, I raise my arm. Loose folds of skin spread from the wrist to the elbow. Disgusting! Where has the beauty of youth gone?

Bitwa asks, 'Do you want something from the market?'

I close my eyes and think. 'No. Nothing.'

'Sure?'

'Well, you are bringing my bangles, right?'

'Which ones?'

'What? Have you forgotten? I've kept a sample for size on the TV.'

'Colour?'

'The same colour as the sari you'd got. The sari's there too.'

'Yes.'

'But don't get me any more saris. They get crumpled from lying down all the time. Just get me a maxi.'

'Cotton or terrycot?'

'It's getting cold, what's the point of cotton?'

He stops at the door. Clears his throat.

'Don't go to the roof.'

Oh ho ho ho!

'And wear a shawl if you get up.'

Ha ha ha! Not a towel?

This time I stop him.

'Listen.'

'Yes?'

'There's a new kind of jewellery in the market these days, what's it called, gold-plated… The real gold ones are lying in the locker… These look real too. Could you get me some, Bitwa?'

How long has it been since I called him 'Bitwa' to his face?

❖

Ever since the women of Laburnum House lined up to complain.

That day it became impossible to get to the roof because a procession of women from Laburnum House – fat, thin, tall, short, straight, twisted, young, old – kept coming down the stairs from the roof into this house's courtyard. It was almost as if our roof itself was falling, and the pillars and parapets and overhangs had taken the shape of women before crashing down, and I'd no longer have even the rooftop to run to.

They crowded around Behen-ji and like always, when surrounded by them, she'd die little by little, little by little, not breaking the image they'd constructed of her, but making it more and more hollow.

All this ruckus because I wanted to buy Premanand-ji's house! I'd even paid an instalment to the agent.

This agent, who was the cultured, respectable son of

a cultured, respectable neighbour. And he was about to commit a grave transgression. Such dealings benefit nobody. There's moral and immoral even in trade. Are we supposed to see her kind of woman becoming a house-owner – and horror of horrors, of that very house – and not say anything?

Behen-ji, you may be compassionate, but the person should also be worthy of your compassion. Is there to be no difference between us and her?

It was essential for everyone's peace of mind that there be a difference between Lalna and them. That she shouldn't be allowed to rise to their level. If she did, people might one day forget where she'd come from. Where would it end? With the destruction of Laburnum House?

The women came to know that Bitwa had asked furiously, 'Where did she get so much money from?'

Sometimes friends also do this – they keep quiet.

'Tell us, Behen-ji.' The moment they said it, I discovered this secret about friendship.

The women kept on muttering and grumbling: She's a bad influence, whether you notice it or not. She walks barefoot and our sons are corrupted. She's started attracting loafers and ruffians to the roof. And our daughters want to wear sleeveless blouses like her.

Yes, there are such women, but they must be held up as an example of what one should not become.

I went into the room so that no one, not even Behen-ji, could see me as I witnessed my own humiliation.

I also went in because Behen-ji too had refused to accept my decision – to buy that house and transform it completely – because she didn't figure anywhere in that dream, nor did her opinion, and the way she'd once given me all the world's courage by rejecting them and accepting me, today she gave the people of Laburnum House infinite courage by rejecting me.

So they started looking at me in such a way that I couldn't meet their gaze any more. What else could I do? Stubbornly hold my head up even higher, until my neck snapped like a twig and my head lolled like Om Babu's?

❖

Behen-ji knew. But not Bitwa, nor anyone else. That now I would not stay. Perhaps she didn't hear their complaints at all. Perhaps she just kept watching me silently, as I silently sat in the room, knowing that we were about to part.

That night the food didn't taste good.

That night, after so many years, we snuck up to the roof to meet.

Climbing the stairs, I'd stop at every step as if pieces of my roof had really come down to testify against me, and the force of their blows still hung in the air, hindering me at every step. Would the roof still be intact?

After the night's chores, it was Behen-ji's turn to come up. Bitwa must have switched off the lights and she must have headed towards the stairs from under the dim bulb that stayed lit all night in a corner of the courtyard.

These stairs.

Perhaps her soft footsteps also felt the hindrance?

She came up in the dark, the way the shadows of the breeze float up.

I used to sit on some other part of the roof, but for now I'll just stop here. And come you shadows, you come too.

We never sat here. Whose house is below me? Who has

made this gazebo out of a tin roof propped up by bamboo sticks, with bougainvillea creeping over it…

How nice! We call it 'baygunbeliya'. See how it's been planted in a big, broken bathtub? As if it doesn't care and will blossom wherever you put it.

There's a washbasin here. And a commode. All the broken ceramic fittings for a bathroom.

Where did we sit in those days? Come, today I'll sit on this broken commode. Pink flowers fall. Their petals are scattered below.

The first of the winter winds. A shiver runs up and down through me.

Behen-ji, why don't you sit on the other commode?

Two shadows swaying in the dark of winter, lighter than darkness, but darker than light… Girls made of thin air.

Who had come to hurt each other, to scratch at old wounds, sad that they were about to part, angry that one of them would have what the other would be deprived of.

No two people can be so close that their lives become one, or can they?

Did we cry? When we cried we always tried to cheer each other up.

But when we laughed, we'd immediately try to make the other cry – because how could you laugh without me?

The leaves of the baygunbeliya kept falling upon us.

Behen-ji, jealous as was her wont, because Lalna was about to make another huge leap, kissing this roof goodbye, onward to a new sky!

'How terrible you must have felt when your own son rejected you.'

Such heartlessness – trying to rob me of my happiness by making me jealous.

'Is this going to be your fate? To be scorned by your own people?'

I had forgotten everything, she started reminding me how I had been cast out again and again, revisiting every little incident.

'And you're stuck here. You won't be able to come away with me, leaving your son behind.' I struck back with the double-edged sword of pity and spite.

We sat facing each other and kept bringing up the forgotten past, we kept uncovering and reopening each other's old wounds – we have become very close, we know each other's every sorrow, and we know that she knows mine and also know that I know hers, and we fear each other like rivals – and we're scared by the thought that once we move away from the safety of each other's gaze, we don't know what we'll do with that stack of unfulfilled wishes the other leaves behind, and with how much rancour we will tear it into shreds.

So we sat that night, with lots of suspicion and lots of tenderness.

And we've come to sit here again today, and our commodes are like the two ends of a seesaw – Behen-ji goes up and, to rise to her level, I push my feet against the ground, and then I rise above her as she goes down…

Two commodes… the seesaw of friendship… so close… reaching out to each other… but we don't touch… can't touch… Death stares out of our eyes…

❖

When the sickness goes, people return once more to their silent abyss, as if these silences alone are healthy. As if what was said was just a part of the sickness – it had to come, and now it's gone.

When I went to keep the thermos of tea by his bed in the morning, he couldn't help but blink, and he looked so embarrassed, as if his heart was reproaching him – You started talking to her? Because of whom demons of unhappiness and disgrace constantly hover over your head, and may at any moment confront you?

The cuckoo sings every day. Have the seasons stopped changing? Or have they moved forward? Or back?

It seems as if something will appear in the air, glittering, glimmering, but no, that's gone too. A slight chill, the harbinger of Diwali, can be felt by those who know how to feel it.

I sit at the table and prepare breakfast for myself. I've reheated last night's pea-paranthas. Ah, the taste of leftover paranthas! I'll have them with freshly churned butter.

Bitwa will eat after I've left the table. That monkey doesn't know how to appreciate butter and cream – pickles are as far as he'll go.

We'll eat separately again.

The old equations seem to be back in place.

Can you tell me, Bitwa, is life moving ahead, has it stalled, or is it going backwards?

A piping hot parantha, and a dollop of butter on top. Roll it the way a paanwallah rolls a paan. Pick it up – oh it's hot, hot, hot – toss it from one hand to the other, blow on it, let the tongue wait expectantly. Oh my, here the butter starts to melt, there your mouth waters – no need to hurry, madam, gone are the days of khichdi and soup, only delicious food for you now – set it upon your tongue like a meditating yogi, let it melt in your mouth, let it slide down your throat, let its molten flavours run in your veins…

Oops!

The damned cuckoo sang out and startled me – and there went half the parantha.

The cuckoo that won't show itself, nor will Bitwa point it out to me.

There is a wound inside me, I know. And if I don't revel in all that's delightful, it will pounce on me with jaws wide open.

What's the point of wallowing in my sadness? It will only leave a bad taste in my mouth.

Better to stay in the country of buttered paranthas.

Bitwa must have had his bath. The wafting fragrance of shampoo announces it. He'll fling the wet towel carelessly on a chair. When he comes here, I'll go to his room – after all, it's me who has to hang it out to dry. Even the fading colour of the wooden chair doesn't bother him.

He's ready. And so am I. To follow our predetermined trajectories – I'll go there, he'll come here. We have to work together, even to stay apart.

I get up.

There's a knock on the door. The doorbell rings.

As I turn, towel in hand, the maid opens the door.

Satchel, bald head, leather shoes, dhoti… Oh dear, it's that bore!

Who'd pester Behen-ji for donations, claiming his cow-shelter was a school.

I react with the reflexes of a soldier at war. About turn, throw the towel, forward march – left, right, left, right.

Bitwa's already at the table for breakfast and is serving himself a parantha.

I snatch it from him, put it back in the container and slam the lid shut.

'Don't let him sit and don't say a word or he'll latch on to you, and he'll eat all the paranthas and beg for stuff to fill his satchel with and ask for money because Diwali's coming,' I instruct Bitwa in one breath and pull up a chair to sit with him.

By the time the maid brings that oily character in, we've composed our expressions in a manner that suggests he has disturbed us while we were really busy, even though it's obvious that we've been sitting idly, surrounded by dishes and containers. The smell of coffee creeps in like a thief.

'You?' I am extremely civil.

'Your aunt?' When he asks Bitwa, smiling from ear to ear and baring all his teeth, I aim a kick under the table. If Bitwa speaks, all will be lost. Only I will speak. Because how can he sustain a conversation with me – I'm invisible!

'She's no more,' I say.

His smiling jaw drops. He has to look at me because at such a moment one hears better with one's eyes.

'She's dead,' I clarify.

Silence.

'What?' He has to ask me.

'Dead. Four months.' Do I need to demonstrate by rolling my eyes up and falling to the floor?

Silence.

He must be thinking: How do I play this now?

Silence.

He must be worrying: Will I have to leave empty-handed?

Silence.

I can read his thoughts: The son will at least offer me tea, and then…

Waiting.

This too has turned into a game, where Bitwa and I have shut our mouths tight as boxes and sit alert.

Waiting: Will I have to leave empty-handed?

Silence.

Useless to wait. No one's saying anything. Even the shameless need some reason to keep waiting shamelessly.

The cuckoo sings.

But I will never see it!

He gets up and we turn as though we'd forgotten he was there.

'I should be going.' He seems shocked. 'I didn't know…'

We stay silent as statues, lest we give him an excuse to stay on.

The maid opens the door.

He's at the door, his back towards us. Our breath is waiting to escape in one endless sigh of relief, and the moment the door starts to close, it explodes in a burst of laughter!

For a second his startled eyes turn to look at us laughing unrestrained, before the door shuts him out completely.

III

He turned, startled. They were both laughing! He was shocked by such merriment in a house that had witnessed death not so long ago. He hurriedly closed the door, as if he'd just taken a bath in the Ganga and the laughter would make him impure again, like a splash of mud.

A mud-splashing laughter!

The stains of which he spread all over the mohalla. It was incredible, people thought. There couldn't be laughter when someone had died. It wasn't just a display of ingratitude, but something more.

The result of this was that the house which had ceased to interest them all these years became, once more, the centre of their attention. The laughter was like a drug that reanimated this comatose story.

A new twist to an old story. A new generation hears it with renewed interest. This woman who had returned – built like a tank, and with no sense of propriety – had come years ago, and as suddenly, as a frail girl with two fat ponytails swinging on either side of her apple-shaped face. Since then, you could always see her on the rooftop, by day or by night. Belonging to no home or hearth, just to the roof.

The children repeat: Belonging to no home or hearth, just to the roof.

The new people ask: But who had lived there earlier? Where did they come from?

Where did they come from? People always come, from this place or that. They come, they settle, they push the earlier ones out.

Oh dear! And that young man, what's his story? Always hanging around her silently, always watching, like a goat about to be butchered. Who is he? The nephew?

Let it be, the elders, still affectionate, say to spare the nephew. And in the tradition of Laburnum House, if you're told to let it be, you let it be. If they don't want you to speak of something but you still do, they'll cut out your reckless tongue and hand it to you! The nephew belongs to Laburnum House, and that is that.

Let his story be.

What story?

Didn't I tell you? Let it be!

But the house – is it his?

Can't you see? His Uncle and Chachcho left everything to him in their will.

And the two ponytails that have turned into a tank?

She doesn't belong to that house, can't you see?

We see, yes, yes, we see. She just goes and sits on the roof.

And what does she do?

Flings her sari, lifts her blouse, and scratches and scratches her back against the parapet.

So, you see, she can't belong to that house.

But we've heard that she's rich. The youngsters are restless, foolhardy.

It makes the elders' hearts pound. What will happen if their innocent curiosity turns into envy?

Who knows where she got that money from? If she has any. Nowhere good, that's certain.

But those whose tongues have loosened will talk. The one who died, wasn't she her friend?

Friend? What does that mean? Good people are polite to everyone.

Whatever it is then, she sure is lucky.

Lucky? The conversation is again headed in a troublesome direction.

God knows where she came from – and look at her now!

She came from nowhere. People like her belong nowhere. They get nowhere.

The elders are worried about their children. What if they start desiring such luck, what will they want next? The good fortune of a weevil in a granary?

Yes, there are people like her, but they don't belong anywhere. Was she able to stay here earlier? Will she be able to now? Don't believe everything you see. Her leisure isn't leisure. Her luck isn't luck. People like her keep drifting, and set others adrift as well. They wander, without direction, without purpose.

Belonging to no home or hearth, just to the roof.

Just hear her laugh, it will tell you everything.

Have you heard such laughter?

That visitor has. He'd come to meet that poor woman who passed away, not knowing that she'd passed away. And he didn't find a house in mourning, but something else. And this woman.

She wears lots of gold bangles.

Up to her elbows.

Even in mourning.

She puts sandalwood and turmeric paste on her face.

Even in mourning.

She puts henna in her hair.
Even in mourning, and she wears it loose.
And laughs.
Even in mourning.

❖

Such was the gossip doing the rounds a fortnight before
Diwali. Lots of mud was being raked enthusiastically,
especially on the roof. Some homes still stood unpainted and
old plaster, cement and lime flew from hook- and spatula-
like instruments, turning into white dust under the waning
moon. Labourers, ladders, rope and wet paint-buckets still
lay on the roof, but flowing between them was a river of
colourful light bulbs, unstoppable in its aim of making the
moonless night shimmer.

People noticed Lalna pacing up and down amidst the
Diwali preparations, wearing a gold-bordered Banarasi sari,
her hands behind her back. As if out to inspect the placement
of light bulbs, candles and fragrant oil lamps. As if Lakshmi
and Ganesh sat in her heart, along with heaps of sweetmeats
and fireworks ready to go off.

As if there was no mourning! She would stop pacing
sometimes, take off her slipper, and caress the roof with her
bare foot – as if petting the neck of a cat – with such dignity
and serenity that you'd think the death in that house had been
a beautiful conclusion, where all of life's sorrows were at an
end, and now the day to celebrate happiness had arrived.

❖

When the strange, heavy sounds of wood and metal rose
from that house on Dhanteras, as the roof was being washed

clean, people were sure that judgement day had arrived. The slam-bang of iron and wood stopped the hands of the women and servants, stopped the children's feet and pricked up the men's ears.

Heavy things are being dropped and moved. Where?

There.

There?

Yes.

A crowd gathers on the roof to look down into the house's courtyard.

As if it's a stage and they're watching a play, while Lalna stands in the spotlight like a ringmaster. And at the back are the rooms where the previous play's props and characters and deaths are stored.

Right on cue, the big, old pieces of furniture start coming out of those rooms like actors in the play.

There's the iron bed from Uncle's coma, walking out upright, with two bare feet below and two hands on either side.

And there's the grand old bed, with its forelegs raised and its weight balanced on the rear legs, walking out arrogantly. If you want to sleep on it, you'll have to hang from it like Jesus.

The clothes rack from the bathroom and the wooden stand, on which Uncle's umbrella, raincoat and hat used to hang, walk out together like friends, dragging a thin-legged labourer between them. The labourer's face is screwed up, as if the wood still reeks of sickness.

The easy chair has turned into a horse and is pulling a labourer onstage, like a cart.

The fat, iron trunk. If it opens its mouth, a blanket and quilt will peep out from under the mothballs.

And the iron cupboard, coming out screeching and limping on three legs, with the fourth lifted up as if in pain. Some gold thread must surely lie coiled inside it. The metallic smell of zari will surely curl out from it.

All these actors from the play gather around Lalna like devotees.

Has the director given some command? Another actor walks out of the rooms and stands in the verandah, a link between the stage and the backstage. It's the nephew. Watching Lalna with narrowed eyes, as if he'd stop her if he could, but since he can't, he won't even try. Instead, he stands quietly.

Action! Lalna picks up a broom and starts mercilessly thrashing the wood and iron actors gathered onstage, twisting an ear here, pulling an arm there. Wham! Bam! As if beating out a ghost.

If the courtyard is a stage, Lalna is an exorcist. As her whacking and thwacking raise clouds of smoky dust, the spotlight shifts to the nephew standing motionless at the back.

Action!

He starts running around the stage, opening up the doors and windows to all the rooms, as if by doing so he'll be able to bridge the gap between the stage and the backstage areas.

The wind makes a rowdy entrance with the opening of the windows. The wind comes, the smoke spreads, the dust rises, the noise intensifies.

And in the centre of the courtyard, surrounded by all the furniture, stands Lalna.

Every article from this house in mourning lies around her, haphazardly, one on top of the other, upside down here, on its side there. And she stands in the middle of it all, as if about to light somebody's funeral pyre. Or perhaps her own.

....

A Conversation between Geetanjali
Shree and Rahul Soni

⋅→⇛⊙   ⊙⇚←⋅

RS: The title of this book in the original Hindi is *Tirohit*, which means something that's hidden, or has vanished away or, perhaps, been suppressed… What I liked was how that theme found multiple resonances, in the way you chose to narrate the story, in the structure, in the characters themselves (who have vanished, hidden or been suppressed in various ways), in how there is so much subtext, so much unsaid that the reader has to grasp at and fill out on his/her own, how almost everything happens offstage and comes to us only through the obsessive recollections of two unreliable narrators. How did you arrive at this method? Were there other ways in which you had tried to tell this story before settling on this one?

GS: I like your saying 'unreliable narrators'! Actually there is nothing like a reliable narrator. Or, indeed, even a reliable author. But this book seems to not mind that at all; perhaps it even celebrates the unreliability of its narrators. There is no omniscient author; the two narrators put their own stories together, not with any intent to lie. As stories/memories get reconstructed and rearranged, something must get left out and something must get added on.

Yes, I like the title – *Tirohit* – and its various resonances. The title always comes to me after I've finished writing the book. The way the various 'hiddens' would have unfolded in the course of writing this novel, is what must have led to the title.

Tirohit is about the multiple meanings that any space has, and any reality. People are too quick to see things in clear divides even as, in fact, many things go on together and may remain invisible.

Here it is significant that women are central to this story. All the connotations of 'tirohit', 'hidden', apply so much to the reality of women's lives. So much of that reality remains unseen, unheard, and merges into the dark, the unremembered. Also, so much is lost to that procrustean 'male gaze' (if I may again flog the much flogged horse!) which, without realising what it is doing, keeps fitting into its habitual cognitive modes even things that are completely at variance. There are instances in the book where two women are together, but the people can only see a male and a female; or peeking down into houses, the youngsters see what they are conditioned to be excited by and not what really is there. Like the scene in which one

Born in 1957, Geetanjali Shree is a Ph.D. in History.

The English translation of her first novel *Mai* received the Sahitya Akademi Award in 2000.

It was also shortlisted for the Hutch-Crossword Translation Award in 2000.

woman squeezing lemons and another mopping the floor are conjoined into a motion suggesting oral sex between a man and a woman!

In peer pressure, if perchance someone sees the actual, they don't admit it. For example, the nephew knows for sure that he slept with his uncle while the two women shared the bedroom, but he does not object when the others say that it was Uncle and the other woman who were sleeping together.

About my method. Well, I do write many drafts. It's always longhand and never cut-and-paste. So the whole process is slow-paced. The form emerges, gradually and indistinguishably, along with the story. I think from the word go it is an exploration – what tone, what form, what story. To the extent that they can be talked about separably – each ingredient makes room for the other, whether in vying or wooing!

RS: Laburnum House is an extraordinary structure, and its roof especially is an extraordinary image as well as a very malleable metaphor – something that stifles and represses when you're under it and becomes a symbol of freedom when you're on it – and yet, not as simple or easy to pin down as just that. Is there a real life model for this?

GS: Today it may seem extraordinary, but it is actually a very common feature of traditional architecture. Many houses with a roof that is or seems one, and on which a parallel life as it were, goes on, in full blast and often wonderfully in opposition to the rules guiding the lives below! It's a space where the forbidden is the order.

So, indeed, there is a real life model for this! Real life models, in fact. We are surrounded by such neighbourhoods, especially in the older parts of our cities and towns – houses under one roof, clustered so close together that you can go from one end to another by just walking and hopping across.

All of Uttar Pradesh, where I have spent many years, has such mohallas. Delhi has the likes of Chandni Chowk. Punjab, Haryana, Gujarat, all are full of vibrant unending *chhats*. Think of the kite festival in old cities, such as Lucknow, Benares and Ahmedabad. The whole city is up on the roof and every roof is accessible, requiring at most a little leap. It is like life has atrophied in the houses down below, the real vibrancy and activity is up above.

Even in other countries – as in Latin America or Morocco, Egypt, Tunisia, to name some – the roof features in a similar way. At least in their films we've all seen it.

Awards and Grants

Writer's Residency
at Romainmotier,
Switzerland, 2008.

International Resident
Writer for the Scottish
Arts Council at Cove
Park, 2007.

Writer's Residency in
Paris, 2004–05.

Charles Wallace
Trust Fellowship at
the University of
Edinburgh, 2003.

Japan Foundation
Fellowship, University
of Tokyo, 1996–97.

Senior Fellowship,
Ministry of Culture,
Government of India,
1994–96.

Indu Sharma Katha
Samman, 1998.

Hindi Akademy
Award for
achievement in
literature, 2000–2001.

Dwijdev Samman,
2004.

Sahitya Academy
Award for the English
translation of *Mai*.

Fellow to the Institute
of Advanced Studies,
Nantes in France,
2010.

And of course, our Mumbai film industry is full of it.

Yes, the roof becomes a rich metaphor for so many ramifications of life. It serves to project an angled vision of a whole society and its moorings, most enjoyably – to me at any rate – of the shakiness of those moorings.

RS: From *Mai*: 'The past is that god – or devil – whom we cannot worship but who is present everywhere, surrounding us inside and out, holding us in its clutches. We are merely a miniscule part of it. We are helpless.' Here again, we have two characters so much in the grip of the past. Is this a constant concern that you keep coming back to and exploring?

GS: It must be, if you have noted it. Since you ask me let me wonder about this. I don't really like to analyse and intellectually assess the subconscious motives behind my creative work. I prefer to live with the image, character and sound that has taken hold of me and go where it takes me, relishing a new journey and the discoveries I make on it. The past per se is not my concern. But I suppose the past or better memory has a powerful hold on us all, whether we are conscious of it or not, whether we give it importance or not. It is a given in our being. We fight it, accept it, or mould it as we go along, knowingly or unknowingly. The past is not a closed entity. Into it flow the future and the present.

The past, in that sense, is often the present of the characters in my works. It presses upon them differently. In *Hamara Shahar Us Baras*, it is a historical past. In *Khali Jagah*, it is a wild, imagined, mad past. In *Mai*, it is a very personal memory. In *Tirohit*, it plays other games.

RS: What prompted you to begin this book? Were there specific images/incidents that set it off? Was it some character? What prompts you to begin any book, and when do you know that it's going be a novel and not, say, a short story or some other form?

GS: Each time it is different. It may be a larger concern, or it may be a tiny trigger. I don't know when I arrived at this method, but I think I let my imagination be, as if in a state of *sadhana*. Ideas, visuals, sounds and memories float in and about, and then some one thing begins to float back again and again. Gradually, it stays. Then I know it's time to be with it, steep in it. Slowly it becomes an obsession, and in strange and unpredictable ways so many roads keep leading me back to it. As I write on, and journey on, that trigger – idea, image or dialogue, whatever it may have

Krishna Baldev Vaid Sammaan, 2012.

Writer in Residence, Ledig-Rowohlt Foundation, Lavigny, Switzerland, 2012.

Geetanjali as a playwright

Adaptation of *Ghare Baire*, bringing out the feminist potential of Tagore's text. Staged in 1989 at the Kamani Auditorium in New Delhi.

Nayika Bhed staged in 1990 at the Prithvi Theatre, Bombay.

Adaptation of Tagore's *Gora* staged at the Shriram Centre, New Delhi, in 1991, as an aesthetic counter to the rising wave of Hindu fundamentalism.

Adaptation of Hadi Ruswa's nineteenth-century Urdu classic, *Umrao Jan Ada*, first staged at the Shriram Centre in December 1993 and subsequently in different parts of India.

In 1998, *Sundari*, a play about Jayashankar 'Sundari', a legendary early twentieth-century theatre artiste who specialized in women's roles.

Adaptation of *Lao Jiu: The Ninth Born*, a Chinese play by Kuo Pao Kun, staged at the New National Theatre, Tokyo.

An Actor Prepares, exploring gender differentiation and movement across genders, staged in June 2002, in Berlin.

Associated with the writing of *Performing Women*, a play weaving together three Greek tragedies, and performed by artistes from Uzbekistan, Iran and India, which was performed in a theatre festival at the National School of Drama, New Delhi, and in Tokyo and Seoul.

Play based on *Hamara Sheher Us Baras*, being performed by the National School of Drama Repertory (2010 onwards).

been – acquires the force of a metaphor. The spine in *Mai*, the roof in *Tirohit*, the round object (bomb or balloon) in *Khali Jagah*, the door in the novel I am currently working on.

My first novel was *Mai*. I only remember that I had no confidence that I could pull it off. But gradually I knew I had to write about mothers who look weak but have some other core that holds them together. I might fail in my endeavour, but I had to write. It was like I was stuck, and if I didn't write that book, I would never get free.

Hamara Shahar Us Baras emerged out of a growing distress over the changing communal climate in our part of the world. It took me long to get started. The fact that it was a terrain explored *ad nauseam* paralysed me yet more, until in a chance conversation the word 'confusion' came up to describe what was going on, and that set me off.

As for *Tirohit*, it was just such a roof and forbidden love affairs on it which excited me. My mood was one of play. There were no rules up there. And with just such a sense of adventure, I played, not knowing, when I began, that two women would meet and form the main plot.

That is the best part of writing – to take dives and find shells and bubbles, and learn from them what vagaries fill life!

I cannot be certain in advance about an idea becoming a novel or a short story. The theme itself settles for its canvas. It may be a large theme, which compresses itself on the shorter canvas, or a more precise, focused tale, which canters along the sprawling field of the novel.

RS: Would you like to talk a little about how you edit or revise your work?

GS: I write many drafts and have no count of how many for which work. I value a good editor, but I do fear the over-dependence on the story-line that concerns too many of us. I do believe that literature is as much about sound, smell, the visual, the intangible, as it is about the content. In fact, the meaning is very much in the cadence of the language a work is written in, in the silences of that language too. For me language is not just the craft, language is itself the story, the statement, the action. An extra word ruins the tale, an unnecessary explanation destroys it. A story is not necessarily 'told', it is 'experienced'.

RS: When and how did you start writing? Did it come about as an extension of what you were reading? Which writers did you want to write like? Every writer has some milestones in their reading career, where

Jeevit Ya Mrit, a play with Seema Biswas in the lead (2010 onwards).

Adaptation of *Dr. Jekyll and Mr. Hyde*, with the National School of Drama (2012).

they come upon a book or an author who expands their idea of what's possible in the medium. What are some of yours?

GS: My mother laughs that I wanted to tell rather than hear stories even as a child. That's far back and maybe it says something about me. But writing is hardly the option Indian parents encourage their children to take up. When they accept the possibility of a girl pursuing a career, they think of other prospects. And that meant that much of my education was geared towards taking me to an English teaching or IAS type line. But I read, and inwardly struggled, being bilingual as many of us are, with the question of which language I would write in. I read a lot of English works, but also, thank God, a lot of Hindi. As a result, both the languages grew in me, however inadequately.

I think there has been a growing fascination with the unstraight route for me, instead of the realism-obsession of much of contemporary Indian literature. And that fascination is not necessarily fed by 'modern' creations. We tend to forget that we come from a tradition where the magical, the fantastic, the unsaid form an integral part of our cultural-artistic repertoire, and of our very existence. Think of the ceaseless transmission of our popular classics – you can't just call them religious – and their renderings into dance, drama, tales, rituals.

There is no one single writer who became my icon. I've always loved writers who chart more than one trajectory together, who write on parallel political and personal planes, like Kundera and Coetzee.

I don't want to go just inward, or just outward, or do any just one thing. I would like to attempt a wider sweep, no matter how small and immediate its range.

Theoretically speaking, it would be wonderful to make a book as eclectic and multilingual as possible. Write in many tongues all at once! It's a dream, which doesn't leave even as we get pulled into our spheres of training and the language we have imbibed.

RS: There is a very distinct sort of idiom and rhythm to your sentences. How did you arrive at it, from *Mai* through *Tirohit* and onward? Is it something you consciously worked on, or is it a refinement of something that came naturally?

GS: I certainly hope so. Like I said, for me language is not a medium to carry the tale, it is the tale. So its idiom and rhythm are paramount.

As for how I developed it, two things come to my mind. One is the way I have learnt Hindi. Mine is not a systematic, formally acquired Hindi. It is eclectic and informal, and was picked up from the vast variety of tongues that characterize the huge Hindi belt within which I grew up, moving from place to place, and of course, also from my reading list that ranged from 'pure' and classical to folk.

The other is my link with theatre, which is almost as old as my writing career. Theatre is a medium which brings together all art forms in one space. I wish to somehow achieve the same in my fiction. I want my writing to be an experience of the visual, the audial, the story content, the props on stage, the gaps as much as the fills making the pattern, an entire *mise-en-scene* making a text. I have internalized this influence, and it makes me see, hear, feel the text as much as read it and understand its content in the abstract. See a colour, hear a rhythm, and not just tell in words it's there.

RS: Elsewhere, you've said that, 'Hindi fiction today is exceptionally vibrant, catholic and confident. It is home to an astonishing range of 'languages', voices, inflexions, styles and techniques. This variety, by and large, reflects the coming together of individual writers with their own distinctive signatures.' Could you talk about some of the contemporary writers who are doing this?

GS: Hindi is a language with very porous borders and into it flow a vast variety of languages and dialects. Plus it is the language of very different regions and also of very different classes and other backgrounds. All these give it a richness that is unique and we end up reading many Hindis all the time, savouring different – even clashing – experiences and sensibilities. There are writers like 'Renu' and Vinod Kumar Shukla who bring their own distinctive locales to make their own 'modern'. Krishna Sobti does it in a very different way. Krishna Baldev Vaid and Nirmal Verma appear more urbane, but the urbanity of one is not the same as the urbanity of the other. Younger writers like Shivamurthi, Sara Rai, Akhilesh, Pratyaksha – to cite but a few from an entire galaxy of distinguished writers – carry forward the diversity.

RS: You've often talked about how writing is a process of constant, multi-directional translation for you. Also, your work has been translated quite a bit. What has your experience of revisiting your texts through translators in different languages been like? And if it weren't for this process of translation, do you even ever go back and read your work once it's been published? Or do you find it more productive to just write and forget what you've already written?

GS: What I've talked about is translation in its many meanings, beginning with the inarticulate being translated into the articulate within the mind, then being translated into words, written or spoken; then there is also the translation of ideas, feelings, sounds.

The translation of my work into other languages is another matter and refers to the more common usage of translation.

In some languages I get to revisit my work through conversations with the users of that language, as in France,

Germany, Serbia or Italy. The questions the readers of those translations ask, the kinds of comments they make, also provide a feel of what the translations must be like. Of the translations in English and some Indian languages, with which I am relatively familiar, I do get a closer idea.

I don't really seek to go back to what I've already written and do move on in that sense. But translations bring it back and generate a dialogue, which brings alive new things in my own work to my own surprise!

RS: What are you working on these days? How do you find the experience of working with short stories different from working with novels, and different from working in theatre?

GS: At the moment two themes are flitting in and out of my head – one is an experience of imprisonment or seclusion on the supposedly wrong side of the border. The other is about a return in midlife, when one is past the rebelling and breaking away of youth, to family and its older, mellower relatives. I have written the first drafts of both, and both are works in progress.

The experience with each work is different, and there is no set pattern that I can indicate about my dealings in different genres. While stories like finding their focus, novels love *bhatkav*, losing the way and discovering!

Theatre is another kind of experience. I like the collective creativity there. It also brings to me the utter malleability of works and the whimsicality of meanings. I provide a set of words, and they acquire other shapes and desires and meanings simply by being spoken by another person, put alongside a prop, placed in a set I had not visualized. It is fascinating how often I find my text acquiring the life of a subtext, which gives the other players of theatre the life-force with which to fly, sometimes rather far away from me, the author – the putative author!

9 789350 296196